Ghostly
Hauntings
of
Interstate 65

Joanna Foreman

Also by Joanna Foreman

The Know-It-All Girl

(Hydra Publications)

Visit the author at

http://joannaforeman.com

Ghostly Hauntings of Interstate 65

Joanna Foreman

Per Bastet

Ghostly Hauntings of Interstate 65

Second Edition

Copyright © 2014 Joanna Foreman

Published by Per Bastet Publications LLC, P.O. Box 3023 Corydon, IN 47112

Cover art and design by T. Lee Harris
        From photos by Joanna Foreman

ISBN 978-1-942166-06-1

Ghostly Hauntings of Interstate 65

Joanna Foreman

Author's Notes

Corydon was Indiana's original state capital and Harrison County's citizens are a proud and loyal bunch of Hoosiers! The first story in this book, The Pink Mystery, was written at the request of *Corydon's Halloween on the Square*, a festival centered around that charming, old city's downtown area on the last weekend in October each year. A stage is erected in the center of the square where contests, live music and storytelling keep hundreds of attendees amused. Booths occupied with various artisans and purveyors of gourmet delicacies surround the perimeter.

The Southern Indiana Writers' Group was asked to create a book of ghost stories with settings on the infamous square, where ghosts have always seemed to come and go at will. The book is titled *Ghosts: On The Square. . . . and Elsewhere,* and a Ghost Walk was presented where authors dressed in costume and followed the crowd to each story setting, reading our stories aloud, answering questions and giving autographs.

I chose the Carnegie Library as my setting and dressed Greta, my granddaughter, in a raggedy pink corpse-costume and proudly paraded her through the Ghost Walk. It was with Greta's permission that I used her photographic image in the story. (What kind of grandmother must I be to set her poor little Pinkie character right on the edge of Interstate 65 on the front cover of this book?) I thank Greta for assisting me with the writing of two of the stories: *MaMoo's Haunted Dollhouse* and *Morgan's Immortals.*

The Southern Indiana Writers meet weekly, and we spent many hours reviewing each story while in draft form — critiquing spelling, punctuation and grammar. Without SIW as my cheerleading section, I may not have found my muse nor the drive to write one story after the other. You may find the group and its many collections of fiction, non-fiction, and poetry (including *Ghosts: On The Square. . . And Elsewhere*) at: www.southernindianawriters.com.

The artistic director for Southern Indiana Writers, T. Lee Harris, lent her expertise to this endeavor with the precise placement of stories and illustrations, and I owe her a special gift of appreciation. Any errors in spelling, grammar, or punctuation can be blamed on her. No, just kidding. But wouldn't it be nice if I could blame someone but myself? By the way, if you find an error, don't waste your time emailing me because I will have found it long before you did, I can assure you! That's what second printings are for, right?

If you find a story of particular interest, tell me all about it at www.joannaforeman.com . I'd love to hear from you.

Joanna Foreman

Contents

Photographs and Photo-manipulations

Marian Allen: Harrison County Public Library
Joanna Foreman: 6, 12, 20, 22, 87, 125, 127
T. Lee Harris 28, 39, 45, 50, 56-57, 73, 82, 102-103
Public Domain photographs: USS Cliffrose p 110, Arlington National
    Cemetery p 115, Dome Cathedral Pipe Organ p 121

The Pink Mystery

On the evening of March 31, 1987, the flight attendant made the day's final announcement: "Ladies and gentlemen, due to the ongoing strike, you will experience a significant delay at Baggage Claim. We appreciate your patience during this difficult labor issue and apologize for any inconvenience. Once again, thank you for flying Delta."

I stepped off the jet way at the Louisville airport and headed for a lounge to kill time. I came close to ordering a cold beer, but decided I'd had more than enough alcohol during spring break. A freshly brewed cup of coffee would better suit me; there'd be tons of unpacking to do when I got home to Corydon.

As I savored the java, I noticed an outrageous headline through the glass window of a newspaper box:

ORANGE GLOWING SPACESHIPS COMMONPLACE IN CORYDON!

The front-page article was short with sketchy details, and wouldn't you know I was fresh out of coins. I was eager to see what all the excitement was about, but when I got home I remembered I had put my newspaper delivery on vacation. I considered calling my grandma, but she goes to bed early, and I didn't want to wake her up. I yawned, reconciling myself to the fact that I was out of luck for the night.

Early the next morning, I threw a load of clothes into the washer and walked a few blocks along Chestnut to the library at Oak and Beaver Streets. A gray-haired librarian, wearing a long, paisley dress, stood next to a cart of returned paperbacks. A large button, pinned onto her collar, read "Octogenarian." Leave it to a librarian to accessorize with a six-syllable word. She directed me to the appropriate department, where I gathered up the last two weeks' worth of newspapers. I seated myself at a large desk and pored through various articles. The news carried a recurring theme: a good number of verified sightings of strange nocturnal lights near Corydon had been reported during March. The credibility of the witnesses could not be questioned because they were all intelligent and responsible citizens of Harrison County. The idea of UFO's as a hoax was not a consideration at all . . . and here *I'd* gone off and missed the entire phenomenon.

I felt, more than heard, a whisper and sensed I was being watched. I looked all around but could see no one except the ancient-and-proud-of-it-librarian, who was busier than ever at the front counter. I shook off the creepy feeling, closed my eyes and leaned back in my chair. What would it have been like to have seen a genuine flying saucer? I'd have loved to have witnessed those glowing orange lights in the sky — something to tell my grandchildren about someday. If only I had been in Harrison County instead of traipsing around Key West, lounging on beaches and watching the sights and sunsets on Mallory Square. Late one night, after celebrating my twenty-first birthday with a margarita the size of a fish tank, my friends had dared me to visit Madam Bellina on Duvall Street, a psychic with an honest-to-goodness crystal ball. I recalled her Gypsy-like appearance: ankle-length black skirt, white peasant blouse and, thrown over her shoulders, a black shawl with hundreds of little silver coins and beads dangling from its edges. She wore a heap of neck chains, rings on every finger and a jingling ankle bracelet. Her make-up — parrot-green eye shadow and black lipstick — was so entirely gaudy that I couldn't take her seriously. As she read my tarot cards, she raised one eyebrow and her face turned to chalk. I wondered if she put on that type of show for everyone who walked through her door.

The memory caused me to laugh out loud, but then I remembered I was in a library, and I quickly opened my eyes to see if I had disturbed anyone. What I saw caused me to nearly fall off my chair.

A pale, pink swatch of thin, gauze fabric floated past me, right in front of my face, and disappeared into thin air! I definitely heard the whisper again . . . *The librarian knows*. . . .

What the librarian knew was a mystery to me. Call it jet lag, vacation let-down, or just an over-active imagination, one thing was for sure — the goose bumps on my arms and the shivers that went through me from top to bottom were real enough. Maybe it was low blood sugar; I hadn't eaten anything today. Whatever . . . I'd learned all I wanted to know about the UFO's. I selected Anne Tyler's latest novel and checked out.

I hurried home to a pot of hot tea, sausage links and scrambled eggs, and reached into my book bag for something to take my mind off the weird library occurrence. There were not one, but *two* books in there, the second one being a yellowed, hardbound historical account of the great Ohio River flood of 1937. I examined the volume and speculated how it had gotten into my canvas bag. The book was stamped on the inside cover *REFERENCE DEPARTMENT.* It should not have been removed from the library at all. Oh great, I thought; now I'd have to sneak it back in past the librarian who knew . . . what?

I transferred my laundry from the washer to the dryer, cleaned up the breakfast dishes and walked, once again, over to Beaver Street. Hoping to make myself invisible, I calmly sauntered past the syllable queen as though I didn't have a care in the world.

"Forget something, dear?" she inquired, squinting above her narrow reading glasses.

"Oh, uh," I muttered. "I think I may have left my pink neck scarf. Have you by any chance seen it?"

"*Pink*, you say? Oh dear," she murmured. "Hmm, no . . . not a neck scarf that I recall . . . umm . . . I'll keep my eyes open."

"You do that, if you can," I mumbled quietly to myself. Her stare bored a hole through me as I walked to the back of the library. Had she seen something *else* pink, as I had?

In the Reference Department I found a spot for the book. Its official title was *Unsolved Mysteries of the Ohio River Floods.* I located the catalog number and tucked it firmly into the shelf, right where it belonged.

After shuffling the few blocks back to my house, I kicked off my sneakers, started another load of laundry and lit a fire in the fireplace. I nuked a mug of hot cocoa and curled up on my sofa with Grandma's afghan.

I'd made my way through the first three chapters of *The Accidental Tourist* when I got up to stoke the fire.

Unsolved Mysteries of the Ohio River Floods lay on my coffee table!

What in the world? Madame Bellina had warned me that something unusual would happen, but don't all psychics tell you that? I had snickered when she predicted it, and at this moment I was feeling just a tiny bit of regret for doing so.

I reached for the old book and thumbed through, reading a few pages here and there, and set it back down on the table. I hadn't realized there were any mysteries associated with the Ohio River floods, but apparently some folks had gone missing and were never found. The floods were blamed, at first, but a prominent theory was later proposed that some had disappeared on purpose, finding the flood a good excuse as any. What a great scheme, if it worked, I thought, but surely some of those bodies had eventually shown up somewhere along the line, probably unidentifiable.

I needed a comforting voice, so I called Grandma to let her know I'd made it home from Florida.

"Did you hear about our UFO's? Oh, you missed it, Honey," she said excitedly. "Walk your pretty little self on down here for lunch, you hear? I'll tell you all about it."

My grandma eats a hearty breakfast at five o'clock in the morning, lunch at two in the afternoon and is in bed by six. She claims that's how she's lived so long. She's sixty-eight now, which really isn't old at all. I'd walk over to see her around two.

I re-stoked the fire, pulled the afghan up closer and settled back into my novel. Before long, I drifted off to sleep. I dreamed of a girl, all dressed up in pink: a street-length cotton dress, gloves and a matching ribbon tied into her

long blonde hair. Her feet were adorned with sparkling pink ballet slippers. She was dancing around the room, singing. Suddenly, she handed me a book, pointing to a specific page.

I awakened with a start. The house was unusually quiet, with only the occasional hiss and sputter of a glowing orange log.

I glanced at the coffee table but the library book was no longer there! *Had this all been a dream?* But, wait. My Anne Tyler novel was on the coffee table, and the Ohio River mysteries book was in my lap! How could *that* be? I was not a known sleepwalker, yet the only logical explanation I could come up with was that I had somehow exchanged the two books during my nap. A strip of faded pink gauze, tied in knots, marked the place of a story entitled "Can Pinkie Find her Way Home?"

Madam Bellina's words echoed in my ears: *YOU WILL HELP A LITTLE GIRL FIND HER WAY HOME!*

Jane (a.k.a. Pinkie) Poppersham, a charming sliver of a girl, went missing the very same day the river overtook much of Corydon's square. It is rumored she was last seen in the library. A fifth-grader and an avid reader, Pinkie could be found there most afternoons after school, doing homework or reading her favorite mystery stories. On that fateful day, Pinkie's mother became aware of the approaching danger of floodwater and ran to the library. As she rushed through the front door and into the vestibule, she noted that the basement was entirely flooded, and brown, mucky water was spilling onto the first floor. The librarian insisted Pinkie had not entered the library that day. The two women worked together getting other patrons to safety, after which time several neighbors joined Pinkie's mother in a search for her daughter until well after dusk, but to no avail.

Poppersham — such an unusual name. I knew I'd seen it before, somewhere. I read a little more of the story, as I was curious where her nickname, Pinkie, had come from. Since she was a toddler, the child had preferred the color pink, and by the age of seven she refused to wear clothing of any other color! Neighbors insisted they had seen the girl enter the library earlier that day. Although her body was never found, Pinkie Poppersham was listed as a casualty of the flood. Foul play had not been suspected.

My major in college is English. The least of my interests is history, and in high school I had truly suffered through those required classes, World History and American History. I couldn't abide the study of Ohio River floods, something that had occurred nearly fifty years ago. Why would I ever want to know about that? Now, I had to admit the stories were interesting, even though I was annoyed that the old book seemed to have a mind of its own, inconveniencing me to no end. I tossed it onto the coffee table and folded my clean clothes.

It was nearly two o'clock. I had borrowed Grandma's set of red crocodile luggage for my trip. I'd return it and see what she thought of the entire scenario. If anyone could remember this Pinkie situation, it would be Grandma.

~*~

In Grandma's kitchen, I opened her overnight case and removed the library book, along with a souvenir — a silver-plated collector's spoon with an enamel design on the handle in the shape of Florida. She kissed me on the forehead and placed the spoon in a wooden display rack on the wall next to her antique Hoosier cupboard.

She flipped up the leaves of her oak kitchen table, and we lunched on Campbell's tomato soup, triangle-shaped tuna salad sandwiches on whole wheat toast, deviled eggs and peach pie. Grandma went on about the unusual sightings in Corydon skies. She knew everyone in Harrison County, so naturally she knew the handful of people who had seen UFO's in their backyards. She said she even saw an orange glow herself. I thought that might be a stretch, but who am I to question her? I listened patiently until she had finished her reporting duties. She seemed happy that I had been away, thus leaving someone she could share the gossip with. Everyone else around here had gotten it firsthand or from the daily news broadcasts.

She stared at me like she was seeing me for the first time. "You needn't be so frightened . . . and pale, Honey. The lights have been gone now for nearly two weeks. I doubt they'll come back," Grandma soothed.

I took a deep breath. "It's not aliens I'm afraid of, Grandma. It's this book," I said as I shoved it across the table. "And the color pink, and the library, and . . . oh dear . . . I'm not making sense at all, am I?"

She looked at the library book and her brow wrinkled. She covered my hand with hers, giving it a few pats. "Start from the very beginning," Grandma said softly.

So I did. I told her about the Gypsy fortune teller, the library, the book and my dream. Grandma was on the edge of her seat and the more I talked the more serious the look on her face, until *she* became somewhat pale herself.

"Okay, now," I demanded. "What is it that everyone else seems to know but me?"

"Why, it's your house. *You* bought the Poppersham house. Check the deed — it's on there. Of course, it's had several owners since the flood. But the house is yours now, I'm afraid."

So *that's* where I'd seen the name — on my deed. "Do you mean my house is haunted?"

"No, I don't believe it's the house per se. I think it may be the library, though."

"The library . . . I don't understand."

"Think about it. Where did you first get a glimpse of that pink gauze?"

"Well . . . the library," I said.

"And the book followed you home, right?"

"Twice."

"Exactly! That must mean that Pinkie really *did* drown in the library, and she has chosen *you* to help her come home, to her family and a suitable grave." She scooted back comfortably into her chair, pursed her lips, and folded her hands matter-of-factly, just the same way she does when she wins at Bingo.

"But. . . ," I argued. "Exactly where is her body? It was never found, you know. If she wants a proper burial she'd better be leading me to her body, I'd say."

That night I went to bed wearing my jeans and a long-sleeved tee-shirt, and I placed my sneakers on the floor so I could easily slip them on. I knew what would happen next, and I wanted to be prepared.

Around two o'clock in the morning, I awakened to find her standing at the foot of my bed. I wasn't the least bit frightened because Grandma had assured me that Pinkie was one of the sweetest little girls she'd ever known. Grandma was seven years older but they'd lived in the same neighborhood and played together often. Grandma had been her babysitter for a few years and confided she'd been devastated when Pinkie disappeared. She warned me of only one thing: "Whatever happens, don't tell your worry-wart mother about any of this. She's paranoid enough about her only daughter living alone."

I stared at Pinkie in the moonlit bedroom for a minute or so. I saw that she had been a beautiful child. She was wearing the same pink dress she'd died in, I supposed, only it was in shreds . . . shreds of pale, pink gauze. She had a silk, pink ribbon in her hair, and she wore pink ballet slippers.

She reached for me and I held my hand out to her. I slipped out of bed and into my shoes. She led me out the front door and up to the library. Along the way she tried to explain how she died and why she ended up missing, but her voice gradually diminished, and I couldn't get a grasp of everything she said. We crept alongside the building toward the back to the massive pine tree. It stood quiet and elegant, with a full moon casting colossal pine shadows all the way across Chestnut Street. Pinkie motioned for me to sit down on a crescent-shaped concrete bench, and she lowered herself to the ground and leaned against the vast trunk.

"Is this it, Pinkie? Is this where we can find your body?"

"The librarian knows. . . ." Pinkie whispered. Then she disappeared. Not in a fast way, but slow like . . . she just

simply faded away.

I sat there for a while longer, figuring out what to do next. I took Grandma's wise advice about not letting my mother in on this secret. When I finally came up with a plan, and I was satisfied it would work, I went back home and slept better than I've slept for a long time. Until five o'clock, when my phone rang. Of course it was Grandma.

"Well?"

"Oh, golly gee. Good morning, Grandma. You woke me up. Can I call you back later?"

"No, you certainly may not. I want to know what's happening to my favorite granddaughter."

"I'm your *only* granddaughter."

"That's beside the point. Now get on with it,"

So I told her the story of Pinkie's visit and our little outing under the evergreen tree. I explained what I planned to do about it.

"Good idea. Now we wait," she said. "Go back to sleep." She hung up.

The next afternoon I was out for a walk and saw a small group congregated around the big, old evergreen tree. The librarian was one of them, and she appeared to be crying. I tried my best not to stare. My plan had worked — so far. A couple of days after that it was all over the news. The librarian claimed she had found what appeared to be a human bone while planting flowers beside the tree trunk. Her story didn't sound at all like the one Pinkie had told me the night before, but it got the job done. The police dug around and found Pinkie's remains, and the following week the Poppersham family buried them in an oak coffin lined with pink taffeta in their family plot. I skipped class and accompanied Grandma to the graveside service.

The memorial was to be at one o'clock, and by noon a good-sized crowd had developed at the gravesite. Behind me someone tapped my shoulder. I turned around and what did I find but my mother's scowling face smack-dab in front of mine.

"What on earth are *you* doing here?" she demanded. "Don't you have class today?"

Grandma nudged my knee with hers, and she spoke up. "I asked her to bring me. You know how fond I was of Pinkie, and I didn't want *you* to miss work."

My mother chewed on the inside of her lip and glanced back at me. "Humph. I'm here now. I'll take over with Grandma. You run along to your classes."

Right about then, in the far distant section of the cemetery, a flash of pink caught my eye, and I said, "Good idea, Mom."

Grandma was shocked, because she knew how desperately I had wanted to attend Pinkie's funeral.

"Come with me, Grandma, and get your jacket before I leave," I said. "And, Mom, save her place . . . she'll be right back."

We hurried to my car and checked to see if my mother was watching. Thank goodness she was deep in conversation with someone. We collected Grandma's jacket, hopped across a narrow driveway and stood behind a large tombstone. In no time, Pinkie appeared. Dressed in an elegant, soft pink dress, she looked very much at peace.

She extended her hand toward Grandma and said, "It's heavenly to see you again, Maggie."

Grandma was all tears and seemed to have lost her voice. "What really happened to you, Pinkie?" she said, finally, her voice shaking.

"You remember Buddy, the librarian's little brother who cleaned the library bathrooms?"

Grandma nodded as she grasped the tissue I had handed her.

"Well, the day of the flood, he was messing around in the basement. He shouldn't have been down there in the first place, but I saw him go down, and so did the librarian. She didn't say anything, an expert, even then, at keeping her mouth shut. Anyway, when the water came pouring in, she stood there, frozen. I figured she couldn't swim, so I bolted down the stairs and into the water to get him. He bobbed up and down and screamed, so I got over to him and grabbed him, but he struggled — panicked I guess — and pushed me away. The water pressure slammed my head against one of those old columns. Buddy somehow got to the surface and just stood there halfway up the stairs and watched me cry out over and over for help. Then, when I went under for the last time, he told his sister what he'd done. That night they dug a hole by the big tree in the back yard and slid my body into it. I hovered and watched the whole thing; it was freaky." Pinkie shuddered. "Buddy was slow, you remember, Maggie?"

Grandma nodded energetically. "Slightly retarded."

"And he talked kinda funny, too, you know?" Pinkie said. "Why, I was one of the few kids in school who *never* made fun of him, and then he treated me that-a-way. Sheesh!"

Pinkie raised one eyebrow and winked. "I've been haunting them both ever since."

Grandma and I looked at one another in amazement.

"Buddy figured out just last year that if he stayed far away from the library I couldn't reach him. But the old gal, well, she just doesn't get it, I guess. She tolerates it like it's part of her punishment, or something. But the thrill, for me, is long gone now," Pinkie admitted.

"What are you going to do about the librarian?" I asked. "She hasn't admitted anything!"

"No, but she's paid dearly through the years, trust me." Pinkie giggled, and then regained her composure. "Besides, what good would it do my family to know the truth? This way they think I was a flood victim overtaken by Ohio River sediment. I got what I wanted. I'm ready to go home, and I can, thanks to you." She turned to face Grandma. "Did you know your granddaughter put a note on that old biddy's front door? Told her she'd better come clean — or else. She signed it Jane Poppersham — in *PINK*." She looked over at me. "A brilliant touch, by the way." She handed me a tiny, gold locket. "My dear mother put this in my coffin, but I'll have no use for it, really. I'd like you to have it."

Pinkie pointed toward the crowd of people gathered across the lawn. "I'd better get over there. Looks like they're about ready to start saying wonderful things about me, and I don't want to miss *that*," she said, smiling, "and . . . *I* have a *soul-train* to catch!"

Proof on Film

There are hundreds of substantiated cases where a form, commonly accepted as a ghost, appeared on developed film, even though no one had actually seen it during the filming. The following is one of those documented stories.

Oliver T. Winston was born on a beautiful, snow-covered December day in 1917. He was raised with his brother on a large cattle farm near the town of Franklin, south of Indianapolis, Indiana. Oliver T. married pretty Miss Evelyn Montgomery on December 12, 1942, and shortly thereafter donned a crisp Navy uniform to serve overseas during WWII on the USS *Cliffrose*. The ship was stationed in Japanese waters and at Okinawa in 1945 and spent the last half of 1946 on the U.S. West Coast, and then served at Pearl Harbor, Guam and the Philippines.

Oliver T.'s tour of duty ended in 1946, and he returned home to Mrs. Winston where they immediately planned their future. It was their dream to add three or four children of their own to the fast-growing American baby-boomer generation. As fate would have it, Evelyn Winston miscarried her first pregnancy, and the doctors warned her she might not be able to conceive again. Fortunately, she did, and the following year gave birth to a daughter, Olivia, named after her father. The precious baby girl was Oliver

T.'s little princess, and, from the very moment she was born, not a day went by that he didn't tell her how special she was.

As his daughter grew, Oliver T. never skipped one single night of bedtime stories and prayers with her. Afterward, he'd tuck her in and promise, "I'll always be here to look after you, my sweet."

Eventually, Oliver T. was offered a position with General Electric at its new Appliance Park facility in Louisville, Kentucky. So the small family moved further south and bought a two-bedroom, one bath, brick, ranch-style home on three wooded acres on a winding gravel road a few miles southwest of Scottsburg, Indiana. Louisville was a good thirty-five miles from Scottsburg, which required an extended daily commute for Oliver T., but he didn't mind, for he treasured the peaceful environment his woods allowed him once he returned home from a long day's work.

Shortly after they settled in, construction began on Interstate 65 less than half a mile from their home. The constant hum of highway traffic annoyed Oliver T., but he ignored it most of the time. "That's progress for you," he would say. "Plus, the new freeway will cut my travel-time in half, and that'll give me an extra hour every day with my two fav-o-rite girls!"

On Olivia's very last day of sixth grade, she hopped off the yellow school bus and skipped into the house through the rear kitchen door. She slapped a spoonful of creamy peanut butter and a layer of homemade grape jelly on a slice of white bread and strolled into the living room. Her father had been working second-shift and should have left for the city already, but he appeared to be asleep in his brown plaid recliner.

Poor Oliver T. Winston. He had died of a heart attack at such a young age, leaving behind a grieving wife and twelve-year-old daughter. Everyone in Scott County who knew and loved him was stunned. Olivia and her mother wondered how they would ever get along without him.

Mrs. Winston found a decent job at a doctor's office in nearby Salem, and they made their way through life as best they could. Olivia often thought of her father's promise to look out for her. She was convinced she felt his presence and set a place for him at the table every evening. Her mother would shake her head in disbelief, and while Olivia attempted to enlighten her to the possibility, Mrs. Winston would hear nothing of it.

Six years later, Olivia graduated from high school and married her childhood sweetheart. They bought a mobile home on five acres one mile down the same road which, by this time, had been blacktopped. Within the next four years, they had two sets of twin girls, and were thrilled when they were able to realize their dream: they replaced the trailer with a beautiful, custom-designed, four-bedroom log home.

Time continued to pass, and Mrs. Winston, now known as MeMaw, had become somewhat frail. Olivia's husband had remodeled their walkout basement into a private apartment, and Olivia invited her mother to move in with them so they could look after her. MeMaw was delighted with the invitation, for the town of Scottsburg had been told there would be a new entrance ramp added to Interstate 65. The Highway Department had offered Mrs. Winston a generous amount of money for her land. Cracker Barrel and McDonald's had designs on the property, as well. She hated to leave her old homestead, but, in reality, she knew she had little choice.

Olivia and her four teen-aged daughters spent one entire Saturday packing MeMaw's valuables, categorizing items for an estate sale. While MeMaw was sorting through her bedroom, Olivia and the girls rummaged through the spare room, the one that had belonged to Olivia as a girl. They unlocked an old, cedar-lined trunk, carefully lifted the lid, and discovered all sorts of memorabilia. Oliver T.'s Navy uniform and the American flag that had been draped across his coffin were carefully folded and wrapped in tissue paper.

"Look, girls, this flag has only forty-eight stars on it! Hawaii and Alaska weren't added until later in the year Grandpa died."

One of the twins decided to try on Oliver T.'s Navy uniform. Olivia watched her daughter with pride. "I remember Grandpa let me dress up in that uniform for Halloween," Olivia said. "I must have been all of eight years old. We had to roll up the cuffs on the arms and legs so I could walk around in it. I'm sure there's a picture of it somewhere. MeMaw always took photos during the holidays."

She dug deeper into the trunk, searching for old photographs. Oliver T.'s Honorable Discharge papers and her parents' marriage license, yellowed — but still readable — were tucked away in tattered linen envelopes. They found bundles of letters tied with faded red ribbon — sent home to MeMaw from Oliver T. while he was overseas. Olivia and the girls read each one as they sat on the hardwood floor, reminiscing. "He told me he would always be here to take care of me," Olivia said, "and he's still around, keeping his promise, that I know for sure." The twins exchanged glances, their eyebrows raised. "Oh, girls, I just wish you could have known your grandfather," Olivia continued. "He was an amazing man." Her eyes teared with the memories.

Just then, MeMaw hollered from across the hall. "Why, lookie here girls! My old Brownie box camera!"

Olivia could just barely remember the camera that had produced all those black and white photographs, most of which her mother had carefully fastened into numerous picture albums, having gotten into scrap-booking long

before it became the rage.

"I'll bet this is worth some money." MeMaw handed the camera to Olivia. "Take it into town, honey, and see what you can get for it."

The next day, Olivia drove all the way to downtown Jeffersonville to inquire at the Click-It Camera Shop. The proprietor carefully examined the Brownie and said, "Why, here's a half-used roll of film in this camera, ma'am."

"Surely it wouldn't be good after all these years, do you think?" Olivia asked.

"You never know. I've heard of strange things with old exposures. You wanna finish out the roll and bring it back?"

Olivia returned to the old homeplace and clicked the few remaining frames, shots of empty rooms, and outside views of the house, too. She doubted they would turn out, but, if they did, it might be fun to have those photos in black and white. Her husband had already taken 35 mm color pictures of the house so the family could add to their scrapbook of memories. She cringed whenever she thought about the place being razed, but, as her father would say, that was progress for you.

Olivia put the camera in the console of her Plymouth Voyager, and had all but forgotten about it, until one day her mother asked how much money it had brought. Olivia explained that it had slipped her mind and made a note to herself to take the camera with its exposed film to Click-It as soon as possible.

A week after the old house had been torn down, the camera shop owner called and informed her the prints were ready. Olivia raced to Jeffersonville, paid for the developing, and, once she was safely in her van, tore open the bright yellow envelope.

There he was — Oliver T. Winston — larger than life. Olivia felt like a time-traveler, seeing these new pictures of her father taken years ago, before he had died. In one photograph he was standing behind her, giving her rabbit ears. *Always the clown, wasn't he?* Olivia thought. Her mother must have realized what he'd been up to, but took the shot just the same. In another picture he was seated at the kitchen table next to Olivia. His plate was clean, Olivia noticed, while hers was piled high with what appeared to be fried chicken and mashed potatoes. In another print her mother was at the kitchen sink washing dishes, while Oliver T. leaned sideways, one elbow on the countertop, his feet crossed. He was grinning at the camera. She couldn't believe her luck that the old images were still good. Oh sure, the black and white was more like dark and light gray, but she recognized him just the same. And of course he'd be somewhat blurry and out-of-focus considering the film had been in the camera for so many years. She put the snapshots back in the envelope and hurried home to show her family.

She pulled into her driveway but couldn't get out of her van; she was suddenly overcome by the realization that her age in those pictures appeared to be at least eighteen — six years after her father had died! She removed the prints once again from the envelope. With shaking hands she observed them more carefully, one by one. With each picture, Olivia could see the images of herself and her mother clearly; it was only Oliver T.'s likeness that was washed-out.

Oh, it was unmistakably her father — the *ghost* of her father to be more exact! In the photo where her mother had been washing dishes, a wall calendar was visible, the year of which clearly read "1965". Oliver T. had died in 1959.

Olivia thoroughly investigated the remainder of the photographs, the ones she had taken the month before to finish out the roll. In each room she could see a vague impression, and yet she recalled all rooms had been empty. Also, in the pictures she had taken from outside the house, a shadow was present at the living room window.

Oliver Winston had been there throughout all those years, until the day the house was torn down, looking after his little girl, just as he'd promised. Olivia knew it all along — he *had* been there for her! For that matter, he was *still* here. She was certain he had moved into her log house once the old homestead had been torn down.

Olivia couldn't wait to show this to her family. MeMaw and the twins would *have* to believe her now!

(See *MeMaw's Breakfast Anytime.*)

Elvis Returns

Officer Otis McCutcheon was the new guy. He'd been on the Indiana State Police Force for one year, and because no other recruits had been added to his unit, his fellow officers referred him as the rookie.

"Hey, Rookie, you seen Elvis yet?" J. D. Bullock, a tall, balding officer with a desk job and a pot belly to match, asked him one Friday morning at the station. Otis had been on his assignment three weeks at the time and had no idea what Bullock was talking about, so he took the bait, "What . . . Presley?"

The other officers snickered; J. D. Bullock guffawed and beat his fists on his desk so hard a glass of iced tea tipped over onto his blotter.

Otis bit his tongue and threw Bullock a look of disgust. He knew the harassment from his co-workers was harmless enough, and he wouldn't always be the new guy. After his shifts, he returned to his little log cottage in Brown County where his wife, Lucia, smothered him with all kinds of attention. Otis, in his blue uniform, all pressed and well fitting.

"Oh, Otis," she would say. "You look so good in that outfit." Why she called it an outfit he could not understand, although he knew that's the way women referred to their own clothes. It was a uniform, not an outfit. A Smokey the Bear uniform. Pants perfectly creased in front, the color of a gray-blue sky with dark blue stripes down each side seam. The shirt was a darker blue, shoulder flaps attached at the neckline with gold buttons; two pleated breast pockets, matching thread sewn along the edges; and his gold officer's badge placed just above the left shirt pocket. The triangular shape of the Indiana State Police decal rested proudly on his right shirt sleeve.

Every morning Otis groomed himself in front of the full-length mirror attached to the bathroom door. He knew he looked better than any other cop on the force. The others were too short or too tall, or overweight, or had any number of other physical detractions. Otis was just right at 5'10", weighing in at 165 lbs. He worked out at a local gym in Columbus three times a week — his abs hard and wavy — especially stunning in his Smokey suit.

Otis had Interstate 65 duty all the way from Jackson County at the Seymour exit number fifty, to north of Columbus, exit seventy-three. He saw it as twenty-three boring miles up and down, all day long. When an emergency call came from anywhere else, say State Highway 46, or even better, Federal 31, Otis wasn't called upon to answer because he had to stay right alongside the Interstate in case there were any emergencies. And there had been a few calls, but when they came in, the other officers converged on the scene en masse, leaving Otis to feel like a fifth wheel every time. So, most days he pulled his patrol car off the road into a clump of evergreen bushes and aimed his radar gun. "Gotcha!" he'd say, and ease back onto the pavement, speed up, flip the switch to activate his lights and siren. The speeders never knew where he'd come from. He held the record for speeding tickets that year.

Otis' assignment changed to the night shift, which he expected to be even more lackluster. Absolutely nothing exciting happened along I-65 during the wee dark night hours. No one was speeding at night. How could they when the Interstate was packed with trucks, Peterbilt rigs, cruising two-by-two? Otis loved to eavesdrop as the truckers conversed over their radios. He knew them all by name: Big Purple Peter, Dream Catcher, Mamma's Toy, and Soul Searcher. He moved around the channels at night to pick up the most intriguing conversations between the drivers. Someday he'd write a book, he thought.

Just past midnight on Otis' first night on late shift, he saw a bright red Ford, possibly a vintage 1968 Mustang model, parked alongside the shoulder at mile marker fifty-three, right past the White River Bridge. He parked his cruiser behind it and aimed a spotlight into the rear of the vehicle. It appeared empty, but Otis had learned appearances could be deceiving. He activated his video cam,

slid out of his seat, and walked up to the passenger side. He directed his flashlight inside and saw no one. Otis tried the doors but they were locked. The pristine condition of the interior, along with the well-maintained exterior, assured Otis the owner would return soon. He noted the license plate, make and model, and called in to see if it might be a stolen vehicle, but it was clean. Otis placed a day-glow orange warning sticker on the windshield: Move it in seventy-two hours or we tow.

Otis reentered the highway and drove along, thinking nothing more of it. People left their cars alongside the Interstate roads all the time. They ran out of gas, or broke down for other reasons. Sometimes it took them a day or two to return, occasionally to find their car on four concrete blocks, but that was not his problem. He wasn't the world's babysitter.

Otis was on duty four nights, and off three, so the following week after being off, he was patrolling his stretch of road around midnight, and up ahead he saw the same vehicle at the exact location it had been previously. He pulled over and once again gave it a thorough check. It was just as before, except the orange sticker had been removed. He called in the license number to double check, but unsurprisingly the results showed nothing out of the ordinary. He reported it in as an abandoned vehicle and made arrangements with Tommy's Towing to remove it. He applied another warning sticker and drove off.

The next morning, a Friday, he went into the station to retrieve his weekly paycheck. J. D. Bullock sat at his desk, same old blotter but a fresh glass of tea. He was viewing the video cam from Otis' previous weeks' pullovers.

"Tommy's Towing says you owe him one. Your *alleged* mustang was gone when they arrived," Bullock said.

"Yeah?" replied Otis, "I guess the owner finally came and got it. Immaculate, vintage 1968 Ford Mustang." The grin on Bullock's face told Otis something was up. Otis thought Bullock should never play poker with anyone but a blind man.

"So, Rookie, have you seen Elvis yet?" asked Bullock.

"Get off my back, J.D.," Otis said.

J. D. snickered, and a few other officers cackled and chortled, and Otis could hear them saying something about Elvis as the office door slammed shut behind him and he headed to his patrol car. *Forget them*, he thought.

He drove through Brown County and up the winding road to his little cabin, where he expected Lucia to be awaiting him with open arms. She had baked an apple pie and the aroma wafted through the opened front windows. He decided he'd have some for breakfast, along with the sausage patties and fried eggs she probably had ready for him. She didn't care what he ate, as long as he kept that uniform on. She sometimes made him wear it to bed, which he gladly did. Otis had heard that cops' wives are born, not made, and Lucia McCutcheon was his prize.

No sooner had he opened the cabin door, he saw Lucia standing at their bedroom doorway, wiggling her index finger back and forth.

"Come here, Otis, I have a new little something to show you."

Apple pie forgotten, Otis hoped she had ordered from the Victoria Secret catalog he had left lying on her vanity with the page opened, the corner turned down to a black, lacy camisole. He had imagined her in it already. He strutted to the bedroom. He would wear his outfit and she would wear hers.

The next couple of nights Otis drove Interstate 65 as usual, and at approximately three in the morning he would pass mile marker fifty-three. He halfway expected the Ford to be there, but it wasn't.

A few nights later along the dark stretch of highway, the red Mustang was parked, again void of its orange sticker. Otis rubbed his eyes and quickly pulled his patrol car off to the side. What in the world was going on? Had his mind been on that black camisole and he hadn't noticed the car those past couple of nights? Why on God's green earth would anyone abandon such a beautiful car? He called in the license number, make and model. He felt foolish repeating this procedure, but it was required.

This time he examined the name of the owner: Wyatt E. Davis. Nothing unusual about that, but here's something I hadn't noticed before, Otis thought. The license plate hasn't been updated from 1968. Well . . . that just has to be a mistake! It would have showed up previously when I called it in, wouldn't it?

He got out of his patrol car to place another sticker on the windshield. When he opened his driver's door to get back in, he heard the familiar voice of a trucker. Soul Searcher was calling him on the CB. "Come in, big buddy."

Otis grabbed his CB radio. "In, Soul Searcher. Over."

"You at this spot every night. You got a problem? Over."

"Ten-Four. Only around midnight. That's when this old Mustang shows up. You know anything about it? Over."

"Ten-Four. You know about Elvis?"

Otis' breath caught in his throat. "That's a negative, Soul Searcher. Over."

"Thought you might need some help with that, you being the new guy and all. Meet me up at the truck stop, next exit. Buy me a coffee. I'll fill you in. Over."

"That's a Big Ten-Four. Over."

Otis drove the five miles to the next exit with his mind full of questions. What does this Elvis fellow have to do with an abandoned vehicle? And why did he continue to bring it back to the same place, night after night? Was a drug deal involved? If so, maybe he could nab the guy and make a name for himself. He hoped Soul Searcher could enlighten him, and the guys back at the station would finally quit pestering him about Elvis. He also considered the possibility that this was a joke the guys were playing on him, and Soul Searcher was part of their nefarious plot.

The two men sat at the bar at Sammy's Truck Stop. The waitress had a cute little white apron tied around her tiny waist. She poured hot coffee into mugs and brought them warm cherry pie with vanilla ice cream. Otis watched her walk away and briefly contemplated how she would look in Lucia's black camisole.

"What I've heard through the years is this," Soul Searcher said. "Back then, White River and the local creeks flooded during the heavy rains of spring. Of course the flooding causes no problem along the Interstate now, since drainage channels were installed years ago. Wyatt Elvis Davis was a traveling salesman. Got that fancy new Ford back in '68, but only had it a week or two when he lost control and went over the bridge. Dang thing landed on its roof and flattened it so bad no way his body could have got out, but he was never found. Some say his ghost comes around midnight to visit that car he loved."

Otis felt a shiver run through his body. He had heard

plenty of ghost stories when he was a kid, but thought they were all hogwash. Until now. He thanked Soul Searcher, paid the bill, left a generous tip for the waitress and went on his way.

When Otis' shift ended in the morning, he went straight to Headquarters and into the computer room where all the files were kept. He asked Donna, the unit's secretary, to check out the accident reports.

"Thirty-eight years back would be in the archives, Otis. I'll have to dig it out. I'll have it for you tomorrow," she said.

The next morning he arrived early, as soon as his night shift ended, waiting for Donna. He circled her desk, jiggling the keys on his belt, and wondered when she was going to finally drag herself into the office. No one seemed to be paying attention to him, so he took a seat in Donna's chair, leaned over her desk and sorted through the paperwork. There it was, a manila envelope with the name Otis McCutcheon printed on it. Exactly what he'd ordered!

He slit the envelope with his pocket knife and pulled out two sheets of paper and began to read: Wyatt Elvis Davis, born April 2, 1945, age twenty-three, had lost control of his car at mile marker fifty-three during the spring flooding. The flooded Interstate had been closed for hours; Elvis had either ignored or had not seen the warning signs, driven on into deep water and hydroplaned. His brand new Ford flipped and landed, just like Soul Searcher said, upside down, flat as a pancake, on the bank of the swollen White River below. An old newspaper clipping in black and white of the upside-down car was attached to the report. Donna had done good work, Otis thought. The article said the man's body was presumed to have been thrown from the car and swept downstream in the raging current, although how it could have escaped from the vehicle was a mystery. The accident happened just after midnight. Heroic efforts to locate Elvis continued for two weeks; his body was never found.

J. D. Bullock had been watching Otis out of the corner of his eye. He marched himself over to Donna's desk. "You see it now, boy?"

"I get it, J.D. I get it. *Now* I've seen Elvis. I'm a believer . . . maybe now you'll leave me alone?"

Officer Bullock laughed, slapped Otis on the back, and went back to his desk. "Oh, by the way, a new recruit is coming end of the week. You need to show him the ropes. We're gonna move you to Federal 31, day shift."

Otis grinned and took the manila envelope, put it into the glove box of his patrol car, and drove home to Lucia.

On Friday the new recruit, Billy Dunham, showed up and rode along with Otis for the next three weeks. Otis made sure they cruised past mile marker fifty-three at midnight, but he didn't say a word about the Ford alongside the road. Curiously, Billy sat quietly in the passenger seat and did not ask Otis why he didn't pull over. Otis wondered if it was possible Billy wasn't observant enough to see the Mustang.

Billy was assigned his own patrol car and Otis began his new route — Federal 31. The dayshift guys all hung out before duty at Seymour Coffee & Donuts and speculated about Billy. When would he call in the make, model and license of Elvis's vehicle? He'd been patrolling around midnight in that area for ten days and still hadn't called in a report. Surely he'd noticed the car by now!

Finally, Otis couldn't take it any longer. "You seen Elvis yet?" he asked Billy one payday morning at the station.

Billy slowly turned his gaze toward Otis and sneered, but said nothing.

A creepy feeling came over Otis and he couldn't get out of the room fast enough. Next day at the donut shop he told the other guys about it. They scratched their heads and tried to figure out why the rookie wasn't playing the game.

A week later Office Bullock, famous for his silly grin, asked Billy, "You seen Elvis yet, Rookie?" Billy stared precisely at Bullock; the chilly look he gave him wiped the stupid smirk right off. The other guys saw it but pretended not to.

Billy was the number one topic of conversation for the next couple of months, not only at the donut shop, but whenever he wasn't around. The guys couldn't figure it out, and it was driving them to distraction. No one even knew where he lived. The only information they had was his full name, DOB and SSN. Bullock told them to forget it, that Billy was a regular guy who appreciated vintage Mustangs. He told the men to get their minds on their work. But they wouldn't leave it alone. They finally had someone follow Billy to make sure he was on the route at the given time. Sure enough, he was, and a few times he drove onto the highway shoulder, behind the Ford. But he never called it in. It was almost as though he stopped to get a look at it and then went on his way.

Otis came up with the idea to have a secret video cam installed in Billy's patrol car so they could keep an eye on him. Turned out, he parked behind that car every night for five minutes or so. Sometimes he'd get out and walk up to the car, open the door and sit in it for a while. Otis wondered why he hadn't thought of that. What a thrill it would have been to experience the interior of a 1968 Mustang, to caress the vinyl seat, take hold of the smooth, wood-grained steering wheel, maybe even turn on the radio. Then he remembered — the doors had been locked!

Billy Dunham, sure enough, wasn't following proper police procedure, and Officer Bullock knew his Captain would want to follow up on it when he got wind of Billy's unusual behavior. He thought he'd get a jump on it, so he called Indiana State Police Headquarters with an inquiry about their unit's newest rookie, the one who had been on the job not more than three months, William Edward Dunham. He requested detailed information: the officer's history, academy training, and current address. He was informed the data would be forthcoming in a facsimile report.

The instant the fax machine rang, the officers on duty tripped over one another to see what it would spit out.

> *There is no record of a William Edward Dunham. He does not exist in our computer system, either as a new or retired recruit. The last officer assigned to your unit was Otis McCutcheon. No other officers have been dispensed from then until this date.*

Otis and Bullock double-checked what records they had of Billy, and they watched those secret tapes over and over. Otis was the first one to figure it out. He hadn't paid attention to Billy's full name before, William Edward Dunham born April 2, 1985. Just like Wyatt Elvis Davis, born April 2, 1945. Born on the same day, forty years apart, same initials, which could have been coincidence, but the Social Security number was the same for each man!

Memaw's Breakfast Anytime

Heading west over the quaint town of Scottsburg, Indiana, a sunbeam abruptly reflects an impressive flash of light off the aluminum frame of a gleaming, cylindrical trailer. Situated directly above the structure, an arrow-shaped neon sign twinkles on and off continuously. Inside the diner, breakfast is served twenty-four hours a day, three-hundred sixty-four days a year.

The interior is cozy, while, at the same time, larger than you would expect. One entire side-wall of the shiny tube-on-wheels has been removed, and a fifteen-foot add-on houses an exposed kitchen, grill, and luncheon counter. The diner sits on precisely the same spot where Oliver T. Winston lived and died, in a house demolished in the mid '80's to accommodate an Interstate 65 ramp and side road. At the far right end of the diner, a galley wall displays, in simple black frames, photographs of Oliver T.'s ghost.

One can visit with Oliver T. two ways: Study the pictures closely, or simply sit yourself down in booth number one. The local townsfolk are convinced the spirit itself can be found, more often than not, in that one particular two-seater cubicle, on the original, trailer side of the eatery, where eight vinyl booths line up against windows. Those in the know avoid Oliver T.'s personal domain, leaving the unsuspecting traveler to experience a delightful breakfast at his own risk — when he discovers, for example, the salt shaker to be filled with sugar, or when his spoon falls from the table, out of the blue. Oliver T. still has his sense of humor, at least.

On the Interstate, Nelson Milligan, a traveling salesman, is daunted to discover his car is apparently running out of gas, and he quickly takes the Scottsburg exit. Milligan stands there at the Mini Mart, fuel pump in hand. He scratches his head and wonders if he had merely *imagined* the stop for a fill-up in Cave City, Kentucky, a mere one-hundred seventeen miles south. He worries about his memory and reaches into his wallet to check his gasoline receipts, but is distracted when he hears the melodic sound of a farmhouse dinner bell. He notices a shiny, old-timey diner nearby, and he figures it must be what had caused the sunlight reflection he had seen as he headed this way. Since he had snatched a simple Continental breakfast at the Holiday Inn in Bowling Green, the thought of an authentic, home-cooked meal appeals to him. He tries to remember the last time he enjoyed good cooking. Surely it was before his beloved wife, Mildred, passed away, a few years back.

The self-serve pump refuses to spit out a receipt, so he goes into the Mini Mart to claim it. He needs the paperwork for his expense report. He compares it to the one from Cave City and is puzzled to see he'd only received ten dollars worth of fuel back there. He considers it a miracle his old gas-hog hasn't gone empty before now, but he swears he had pumped a fill-up. His bad memory again, he figures. His stomach growls, so he pulls his Cadillac into the parking lot next door at *MeMaw's Breakfast Anytime.*

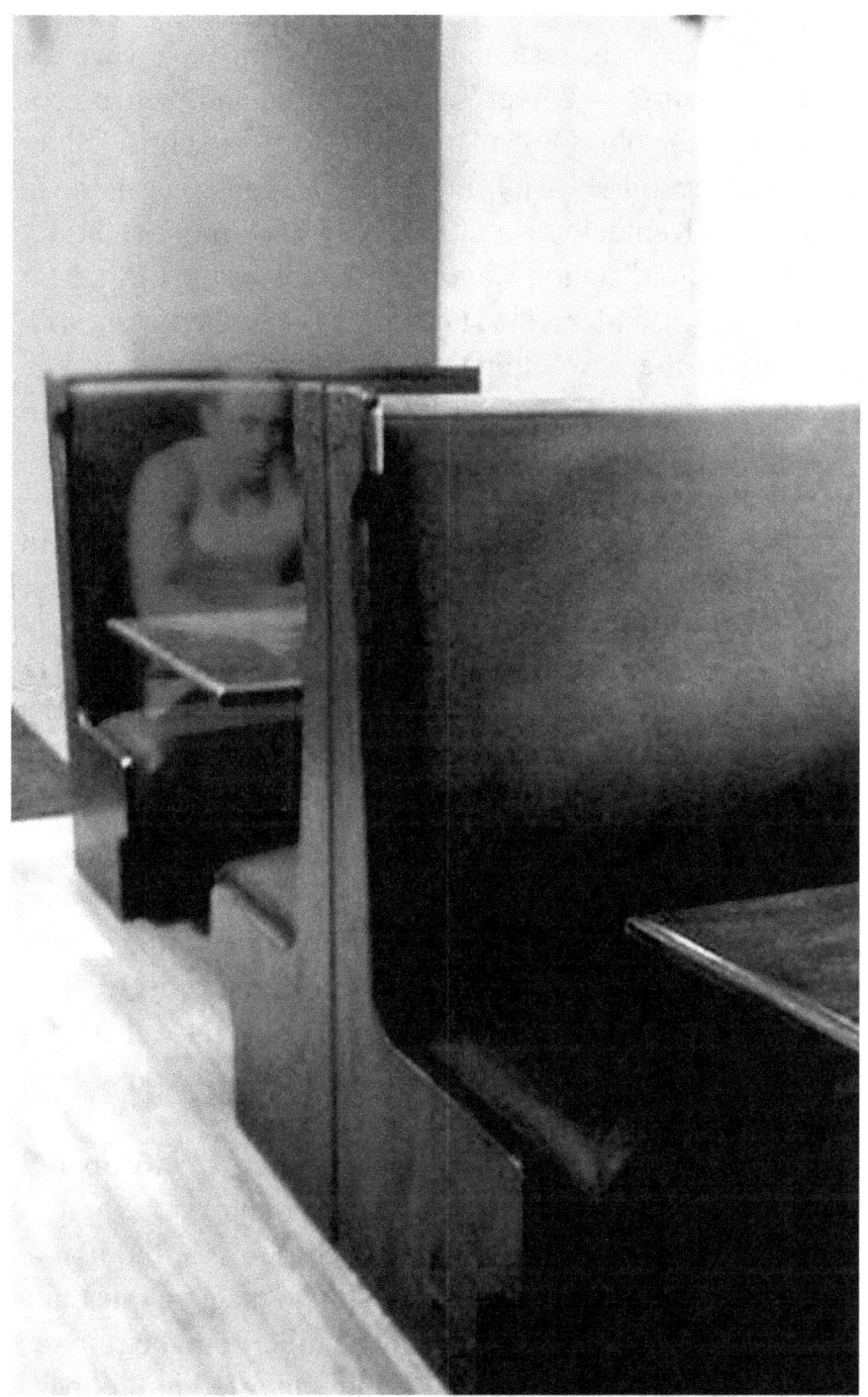

~*~

The idea for the restaurant originated in 1957, when the Winston family — Oliver T. and Evelyn, and their precocious ten-year old, Olivia — moved to Scottsburg. Oliver T. had a second-shift job at the G. E. Appliance Park in Louisville, Kentucky. He clocked out each night at 11:45, steered his Ford station wagon north, across the Clark Memorial Bridge, and traveled up Highway 31, alternating with portions of the new Interstate 65. At approximately one o'clock every morning, he bounded through the kitchen door to the aroma of sizzling, applewood-smoked bacon and homemade buttermilk biscuits.

"Shuggie," Oliver T. would say, "there's nobody else in the whole, wide world can bake up a batch of biscuits for her man like this, in the middle of the night."

Evelyn Winston firmly believed the old adage: the way to a man's heart is through his stomach. She'd discovered that fact for herself early on in their courtship, when she gave Oliver T. a pint-sized jar of homemade grape jelly on his sixteenth birthday. Much to Evelyn's delight, he seemed to follow her everywhere after that. Her parents had owned a fruit farm not far from Oliver T.'s family home, near Franklin, Indiana, and her father's pride and joy was his grape arbor. Evelyn had learned to make jelly, as well as jam from the family strawberry patch, and preserves and marmalades from various fruit trees.

It became Oliver T. and Evelyn's dream to open a restaurant, one where she could put her culinary expertise to good use. Evelyn had never worked outside the home, but, Oh could she bake! Construction on the new Interstate had delivered the highway less than a mile from their home. Oliver T. assured his wife that if they invested in billboard advertising many a man would quickly decelerate onto the exit ramp to savor a hearty breakfast, either before his workday began, or after, as was the case with Oliver T., working second-shift the way he did. They discussed the prospect with excitement nearly every morning while Oliver T. chowed down on his signature meal: four crisp strips of bacon, two poached eggs, fried apples, and buttermilk biscuits slathered with real butter and, of course, grape jelly.

Sadly, Oliver T. didn't live long enough to make his dream come true; he died in his sleep in 1959. But his spirit remained, watching over his wife and daughter, a fact to which Evelyn Winston had been oblivious. Their daughter, Olivia, however, even at the tender age of twelve, had a keen sixth sense, and she grew up feeling surrounded by an ethereal cocoon of security. Many years later, after she married and had four daughters of her own, she was able to convince her mother of Oliver T.'s ever-continuing presence with the help of some film in an old camera. Photographs taken in 1965 clearly showed Oliver T.'s ghost in the background!

(*See Proof On Film.*)

Evelyn Winston was proud as punch to have her named changed to *MeMaw* by four granddaughters, and it was a good thing they were with her the day she first saw the photographs of Oliver T.'s ghost, because she fainted straight-away into the arms of two of the girls. Olivia had run for the smelling salts and MeMaw revived after a whiff or two. You'd have thought she was from Missouri the way she had to be shown that the images were real. Olivia had finally invited a Paranormal Investigator in from Ohio to explain it to her mother. MeMaw called the man a Spook Specialist behind his back.

"Human beings are energy forms, ma'am," he kindly explained to MeMaw. "When the body expires, that energy usually leaves, crosses over, goes on to other projects, you might say. In your husband's case, on the other hand, these photographs are absolute proof that Oliver T.'s energy remained close by. From what your daughter tells me, she believes he clearly intended to protect his family from evil."

"Now, *that* he did a good job of," MeMaw said. "I have to admit." Even for a Spook Specialist, MeMaw thought he made good sense.

"You see, these latest photographs show Oliver T.'s energy has waned through time. The pictures taken last month show that, while his presence remains, it's not nearly as strong as in the early years after his death. I would imagine now that the house is torn down, he has crossed over entirely."

Olivia thought otherwise, but felt no need to say so at the time.

After purchasing MeMaw's property, the Highway Department constructed a new and improved exit ramp, and, in 1990, leased a tiny parcel to MeMaw for the placement of her diner. By this time, she was approaching seventy years of age, in good health and eager to open the diner that she and Oliver T. had dreamed of so many years ago. *MeMaw's Breakfast Anytime* would serve as her legacy, something her granddaughters could carry on, long after she was gone.

MeMaw's two sets of twin granddaughters are twenty and twenty-two and each enrolled in the local college. They work in shifts, waiting tables at the diner, but on this particular morning they are pre-occupied with finals, so MeMaw takes the shift herself. She wipes a table and glances out the window. She notices an elderly gentleman in a crisp, beige suit. He's parked his old Cadillac in the lot and is approaching the front entrance.

Nelson Milligan slides into booth number one.

"You might be more comfortable over here, sir," MeMaw says. She points to the adjacent four-seater.

"No thank you, young lady. I'll remain in this smaller booth. A family may come in and need the larger one."

"I doubt it. We don't begin to fill up after the breakfast crowd 'til noon, and it's not even close yet. Move on over now, won't you?" She notices his business suit, seersucker, it is, and thinks Oliver T. will undoubtedly squirt ketchup on it if he's in the mood. Oliver T. never approved of seersucker on a man — called it "sissified". She had always thought it an attractive fabric, though.

"I'm good right here, ma'am. Thank you," he says. He selects a menu propped up beside the napkin dispenser and proceeds to order. Four slices of bacon fried crisp, two eggs, poached, buttermilk biscuits and a serving of fried apples.

Just like Oliver T. loved to eat, thinks MeMaw. She smiles at the short-order cook as she reaches up to place the ticket into the carousel. On a whim, she turns and takes a seat in the booth, opposite the man, if for no other reason than to protect him from Oliver T. Just in case.

He appears happy for her company. "What's a pretty young lady like you doing in a place like this — shouldn't you be retired by now?" he boldly inquires.

MeMaw feels her face flush, tells him she owns the place, talks about her four twin granddaughters, and how she gets to spend time with them this way. She doesn't know what she'd do without them.

He proudly shows her photos of his grandchildren, all in Florida now, and says his wife passed away, leaving him lonely in his highway travels. They'd motored around together in a small travel-trailer. Mildred had loved second-hand goods and other peoples' cast-offs, so he'd dropped her off at junk shops in small cities, and, while she shopped to her heart's content, he called on his customers. He'd picked her up afterward, and they would carry home a basket, a stoneware crock, or a painted bench, anything primitive. Their son owned an antiques shop in Ft. Lauderdale and he always doubled or tripled their money for them. He says his travel-trailer is now parked in an "over fifty-five" court in south Florida, and surely he could have retired long ago, but isn't sure what to do with his free time.

A bell chirps behind the counter, and MeMaw excuses herself to retrieve the hotplate. Milligan gets up and walks toward the end of the diner to wash his hands in the restroom. MeMaw sees him back there, surveying Oliver T.'s photograph gallery. When he returns, she seats herself once again across from him, with his breakfast perfectly displayed on the table. He takes his seat, and smiles warmly at her. He has a definite look of recognition in his eyes that had not been there before.

"I've heard of this place, but it didn't dawn on me until just now that I was *in* it. Why, you're practically famous! I saw the story on television and read about it in some newspaper somewhere, too, and not a sleazy tabloid, either."

"*Practically* famous? Shucks — I *am* famous! It made the news big time. Folks come from all over. We get all kinds 'round here, believe you me."

"I'll bet you do . . . so you're Oliver T.'s wife?"

"NO, I *used* to be his wife," she blurts out. "I'm his *widow* and have been for thirty-one single, solitary years now. Some day when I reach the Pearly Gates, I'm gonna ask him, 'Which element of *till death do you part* did you not understand, Oliver T.?'"

The salesman laughs. He asks her if she has a dinner bell. Says he heard it vividly, but didn't see one anywhere.

"If you don't see it, it's because I don't own it," she replies. "You musta been hearin' things, old man. Nobody 'round here has one, as far as I know."

He squints at her. He admires a feisty temperament in a woman. He wonders why she's never remarried. Surely she could've had her choice of suitors through the years, spirited as she is. He thinks about the long line of wrinkled biddies that forms at his trailer door when he is at home, all hoping to snag a husband. He takes a bite of bacon, and he shrugs.

MeMaw figures his shrug to mean the whole ghost story thing is no big deal to him, after all.

The salesman is recalling the accounts he's read of Oliver T., the man who chose to stay behind and protect his family. He wonders how Oliver T. Winston will react when he, Nelson

Milligan, courts his widow. Will he allow it?

He breaks open a biscuit and reaches for the glass container of grape jam. MeMaw sits, alert and ready, fearful that Oliver T. will dump it in the man's lap. She hopes to catch whatever spills out before it reaches that nice seersucker suit.

But nothing spills. No silverware drops. And when Milligan picks up the saltshaker, sprinkles a little into his hand and tastes it, MeMaw watches, her brow slightly furrowed. Surely Oliver T. has mixed it with sugar, a favorite trick of his. Milligan salts his eggs, takes a bite, throws another grin at MeMaw and nods. He knows what Oliver T. is up to. He now understands why he ran out of gas at precisely the place he did. He needn't worry about his memory anymore. Oliver T. had crossed over and rung a dinner bell from the other side, leaving the responsibility for his family's protection to Nelson Milligan, a man who would never again travel alone.

The home-cooking would be a bonus.

(See *Oliver T.'s Story*)

Storm Rider

Ordinarily, I'd have hobbled down to the Franklin, Kentucky town square to hook up with a couple of my old Army buddies at the Circle Theater to enjoy a Technicolor flick. But this isn't just any Wednesday. It's nineteen-hundred and fifty-seven, first Wednesday of June, and it's raining cats and dogs. So here I sit, alone, tucked away in this worn, vinyl booth . . . waiting. I can barely make out the green dinosaur on the white Sinclair sign out at the road. The flashing neon *Dave's Bar and Grill* reflects red raindrops cascading down the window, mirrored onto my Early Bird Special plate of meatloaf, mashed potatoes and green beans.

A Harley-Davidson pulls up outside and parks between a shiny new '57 Bel Air and a baby blue Nash. Its rider hops off and bolts for the door. He doesn't even take time to cover his ride, so I know I'm in for a treat. He takes a seat facing me at the next booth. He's pale as a ghost, and I know sure as I'm sittin' here . . . he's seen one!

Peggy Sue struts over to him, flips open her green order pad, and asks, "What can I get for you, Sugar?"

I hold a newspaper up so he won't spot me staring at him. I doubt he'd notice, though, 'cause he's pretty shook up. He's got his head in his hands, and I wonder if he's crying, but more than likely it's raindrops. He's soaked to the bone. Orders coffee. Peggy Sue winks at me as she dashes off to get it. The man reaches for a napkin dispenser and pulls out a handful. He wipes his face and neck, and mumbles, but I can't make out what he's saying.

"Here you go, Sugar." Peggy Sue sets a steaming mug in front of him. "What else can I get you?"

"I ain't hungry," he whines. "Appears I've lost my appetite."

Peggy Sue glances over at me with a wicked smile. "Well, Sugar, you do look a little pale," she says to her customer. "Why, look at you . . . you're shaking! You must be cold from the rain soakin' into your jacket. Maybe some hot vegetable soup would do you good."

"Nah, not soup — it's whisky I could do with. Bring me a double shot."

I see the gears in Peggy Sue's brain go into action as she hurries off to fill the order. She returns in a flash, refills my coffee without a word, then plops herself down in the next booth. She scoots over real close to the damp, pale stranger. "Here's your whisky, darlin', and hot chicken vegetable soup — on the house. Gracious me, Sugar, you look like you've seen a ghost. You wanna talk about it?"

He stares at her like she's clairvoyant or something. He tilts his bearded face backwards, downs the whisky in one gulp, slams the shot glass on the table, and confesses in a whisper that he's afraid just maybe, mind you, he *has* seen a ghost.

"We get that a lot around here when it rains, you know," says Peggy Sue calmly.

"When it rains?" He uses a napkin to wipe his ears, like maybe he's not hearin' so good.

"First Wednesday of any month, as a matter of fact," Peggy Sue says. "When it storms like this, then, yes, we get that a lot around here. Folks in these parts call him the Storm Rider. You did hear the horse galloping, am I right?"

His dark brown eyes widen and his mouth drops open, then he shuts it and gets this real serious look on his face, like maybe now he's thinking Peggy Sue is for real. "Yeah, I was headed south on that brand new section of Interstate 65, out there just before the state line, when the storm hit. I stopped under the overpass so I wouldn't get drenched."

"The old Clark Road overpass?"

"That's the one. I waited for a while, but the storm looked like it was gonna hang around forever, so I shut Suzie-Q down." He nodded his head toward the window, outside, where he'd parked his bike. "Suzie-Q, she's my new Hogg," he says with pride. "Anyhow, that's when I heard the horse pounding the pavement. I thought my ears was playin' tricks on me, but then I saw it. It *was* a horse, by golly! A huge, white stallion from what I could tell. And its rider was whipping at it like a jockey in the homestretch. They went past me faster than a flash of light and vanished right into the concrete wall on the other side of the road. By that time, I thought I was seeing things too. I knew it couldn't be just ordinary thunder and lightning!"

The man glances out the window at his bike, which is getting a good pelting from the storm. He turns back to look at Peggy Sue and notices her nametag pinned to a hankie on her uniform. "So help me out here, Peggy Sue — what's the story?"

Peggy Sue looks over at me, and I duck my head back into my paper, but not before I flash her a wink so she knows I approve of what's coming next. I've heard the story told

many a time. Peggy Sue embellishes it better than most, and here she goes right now into her storyteller mode. You'd think you were reading it right out of a book!

"Well, allrightie, then, Sugar, since you asked," Peggy Sue says. "It's a true story, you know. Was back in 1880, April 7 to be exact, a Wednesday," Peggy Sue began. "A tobacco farmer owned a nice spread just down the road from here. Fancy white clapboard farmhouse, lots of green pasture land for his horses, a real pretty wife and two itty-bitty kids: baby Annie, and the farmer's pride and joy, their firstborn son, Davie. The story goes that Davie had been out playin' near the barn most all afternoon, when one of those quick, spring storms popped up from nowhere. His mother called for him, but he didn't answer. The man went out hollering for Davie, searching the barn and surrounding buildings, but couldn't find the boy. Ominous clouds, then heavy rain and wind, and finally a funnel cloud headed right through the middle of their property. The mother, Caroline, said that's when her husband ordered her and baby Annie down into the storm cellar, and he hurriedly saddled a horse and rode off into the approaching darkness to search for their boy.

"The storm ended as fast as it had begun — you know how spring storms can be. Caroline came up out of the cellar into the restored daylight and looked for her family. Little Davie ran out of the barn crying, arms outstretched to his mommy. He'd fallen asleep in the hayloft so soundly he hadn't heard his father calling, but the intense sound of the tornado had awakened him, they say."

The customer squirms and fidgets. "Get to the point, Peggy Sue. I mean, it's good the kid was safe and all, don't get me wrong, but what about the man on the horse?"

Peggy Sue wrinkles her forehead. She heaves a sigh, and frowns.

I, myself, have learned not to interrupt the girl, as she does hate it so, 'specially when she's in the middle of a story like this one.

Peggy Sue scolds, "Hold your horses. Get it? Hold your horses?" She giggles.

Now the customer heaves a sigh.

Peggy Sue continues. "The neighbors formed a search team for the poor farmer. Well into the night, dozens of men set out on horseback with kerosene lanterns. They found him around midnight, two miles from his home in a ravine down by Robb's Creek, where the tornado's fury had deposited him, still sitting on his horse, all tangled up in the braches of a fallen tree." Peggy Sue puts a dreadful expression on her face, like she's in an on-stage performance. "I've heard tell it was a horrible, gruesome sight," she adds.

Here is where Peggy Sue has inserted fictitious details, but what's the harm? She aspires to be a famous writer someday, so this is good practice for her. Truth is, they weren't found all tangled up in tree branches at all, or at least that's not the story I've always heard from my elders, and shouldn't they know better than little Miss Peggy Sue, here? She wasn't even born back then; she's all of maybe twenty-one years old. Come to think of it, her own grandpa hadn't even been thought about yet! No, my version of the story (and I do believe it is accurate) is that the farmer and his horse were found lying peacefully at the edge of Robb's creek. They'd had ample time to travel those two miles on horseback, so it's doubtful the tornado had picked them up and carried them there. The horse had lost its footing and fallen into the ravine. Now, that's the honest account of the tale. Some folks say there was, in reality, no actual tornado at all, merely a severe thunderstorm. I like that version even better. It pains me greatly when I picture that man and his horse, flying through mid-air, coming in for the vicious landing that Peggy Sue likes to describe.

Peggy Sue continues, "Ever since that fateful night, the ghost of the farmer and his horse return to the scene on the first Wednesday of each month, but only if it's raining. They search in vain for Davie, who, thankfully, wasn't lost at all, which you've already so benevolently pointed out."

There she goes again. Peggy Sue likes to use big words, not only to impress people, but to offend them as well. Dennis doesn't seem to notice he's been insulted.

Another bearded motorcyclist swaggers through the doorway and takes a seat at the bar across the room. "Can I get some service over here?" He looks as pale as a ghost.

I, myself, have attempted to see the Storm Rider on numerous occasions, but he's never shown up for me.

Peggy Sue slithers out of the booth, rips her customer's check from her order pad and hands it to him.

He pulls a few bills from his wallet. "That poor Davie kid," he says, shaking his head. "I wonder if he grew up knowing he was responsible for his father's death."

My blood turns cold. I'm glad to see him gather up his change after Peggy Sue brings it back. Don't surprise me none — he doesn't leave her a tip. He mounts Suzie-Q and they roar off the gravel lot, headed toward Tennessee, no doubt vowing never to return to Simpson County.

Peggy Sue clears away the empty whisky glass and untouched soup bowl. My tight lips quiver as I form a smile just for her, and I neatly fold up my newspaper. She smiles back at me with that sympathetic look of hers. She places a man-sized helping of hot cherry cobbler smothered with homemade vanilla ice cream in front of me, lightly pats my shoulder, and says, "Don't pay him no mind, great-grandpa Davie. Nobody around these parts is fool enough to blame a three-year old kid for falling asleep in his father's barn on a warm, spring day."

The Painted Lady

A few years ago, while traveling south on Interstate 65 from Louisville to Nashville on a business trip, I stopped for lunch at a café in Cave City. Like most writers, I have a tendency to eavesdrop to stimulate the muse. Ears tuned, pad and pen at the ready, I selected a table in the center of the restaurant.

"Darn if I didn't see her again last night, Shirley," said a man seated at an adjacent table. "She motioned me off the road as usual. Of course, when I took the exit there was no one there. Big surprise, right?"

"Seems to me you'd learn to ignore that ghost of yours," the waitress chided as she refilled his coffee. "You should know by now she's never gonna be there." The waitress busied herself with another customer.

I'd heard the word *ghost,* and, while I wasn't looking for a ghost story, it seemed one had found me. That had been happening a lot lately.

"Psst," I whispered, as I leaned over cautiously toward him. "Excuse me, but did I hear you say you've had a ghost giving you highway directions?"

The man glanced at me and chuckled nervously. "Yeah, whenever I travel this portion of the Interstate at night, she's up there on the overpass, gesturing like a wild woman. I think maybe she wants my company for the night . . . she's dressed pretty skimpy, if you know what I mean," the man admitted with a slight look of guilt.

"Who *is* this woman?" I asked.

"I don't *know* her," he insisted, "but everyone else around here says there's a spirit of some kind on that overpass. Some say two or three, but it's all hearsay — something to do with graves disturbed during Interstate construction years ago. That's all I know about it."

After I completed my business, I returned to Cave City so I could spend some time around town — do a little bit of research on this fellow's tale. First, I visited the café where Shirley, the waitress, filled me in on a few of the details and told me where I could get the scoop. A truck stop down the road, she said, would be full of Teamsters only too happy

to report what they'd seen and heard.

I talked to several drivers that afternoon. A few guys admitted they had seen a scantily-clad lady on the overpass late at night, motioning for them to pull off the road. They chalked the sightings up to being tired or teenagers playing pranks.

One of them suggested I speak with Chuck Long, an old man well-known for spouting incessant nonsense about a hooker his grandfather once kept the company of. "He swears the lady's ghost haunts that overpass. Most of us think he's full of hot air," the trucker said, "but, hey, you never know. What've you got to lose but time?"

I had three days, and I figured that should be plenty. I mean, how long could Chuck Long talk, anyway? The problem was, no one knew exactly how I could find him.

In my hotel room, I ordered pizza delivery as I browsed

the Cave City White Pages. There were three Charles Longs in the telephone book. The first guy I called answered in an elderly, firm voice, "Chuck here." I told him I was researching the local apparition and was looking for the Chuck Long who could answer my questions.

He laughed. "Yeah, it's a hooker's ghost all right," he said, and I could almost hear him smiling across the wire. He agreed to meet me at the café for lunch the next day, his treat, he said.

Bingo! How easy was that?

The next morning I visited the community library and the local police station. One uniformed officer told me to pay no mind to Chuck Long. "He's harmless enough, but crazy as a loon."

Everyone else I spoke to was helpful, although I'm not convinced they were entirely truthful. People have a tendency to embellish when it comes to ghost stories. I took whatever tidbits of information I could get, grateful for the input. The story came together like a jig-saw puzzle, one piece at a time.

The Little Church of Saints, a non-denominational group, (or what was left of it, I should say) sold their church to the Highway Department in 1960. The Saints had congregated for twenty years or so in a small, wood-framed house of worship.

The original structure, a two-room cottage, had been built in 1854 by a Madam and her elite selection of girls. The *ladies of the night* had claimed to be Madam's cousins visiting from up north in New England. They stayed to themselves and kept their true profession hush-hush. Women-folk in nearby communities were unaware of what really went on in that little house, and men-folk (the clientele) kept the secret for obvious reasons.

A Baptist congregation bought the house in 1905, indifferent or unaware of its history. They put a fresh coat of white paint on it and added a vestibule in the front. A lone outhouse sat back about one-hundred feet behind the dwelling, and they gave it a coat of paint as well.

Some years later, the Methodists took it from there. They painted it, too — dark green with white trim — and topped it off with a magnificent steeple.

The story goes that a Church of Christ congregation used it for countless years. They painted it sky blue and added stained-glass windows designed with a cross in the center.

Throughout its history, from what I could gather, nearly every religion laid claim to the building except for the Catholics. In due course, even a Jehovah's Witness congregation bought the church. They painted it taupe with dark cocoa trim and promptly removed the steeple which was a pagan symbol, according to their doctrine.

Each of the previous congregations had sold the building to the next because their flocks had grown, and the church was too small to contain them any longer. When Jehovah's Witnesses outgrew the building, they sold it to the Little Church of Saints in 1940.

The Saints didn't think it needed re-painting, nor did they care that the steeple was missing, but they insisted on indoor plumbing. They used the house regularly for another two decades. Eventually, the parishioners, rather than growing as an organized group like the others before it, dwindled down to nothing over some trivial issues — no one seemed to remember what they were. The few worshippers who remained met every Sunday in their preacher's living room.

The fact that Interstate 65 was planned through the Cave City vicinity had been well established years before the bright yellow bulldozers showed up. Local property owners had received genuine offers to sell, and much of the area sat empty for quite some time before the freeway's actual creation, somewhat like a ghost town. My story centered on one small frame building, now gone and mostly forgotten.

The church was abandoned approximately five years before the Interstate flattened it. In the meantime, the outhouse had crumbled with age, and literally dissolved into the ground. The yard was a hodgepodge of overgrown weeds and fallen tree limbs, interspersed with a medley of trash and dead leaves. The middle of the roof sagged precariously — weakened when the steeple was removed.

The house had been painted with so many different colors throughout the years that, even though she wasn't a Victorian mansion, she eventually came to be called *The Painted Lady* by her neighbors. Chuck Long laughed at the irony when he told me this at lunch that day. He'd lived in the region for over sixty years. According to Chuck, some people thought the fresh coats of paint were whitewash ceremonies — to cast sin away — sins committed, mind you, by the *former* religious group.

"If that's the case," I said, "I'd be curious to know what they did to the *inside* to get rid of the metaphorical cooties, if you know what I mean."

Chuck enthusiastically nodded in agreement. He didn't seem crazy to me, but he was a little difficult to understand because he had no teeth. I interviewed lots of people, but Chuck was the only one who knew the house had been a brothel. It occurred to me, at first, that he, himself, had invented the story.

At long last, the Interstate made its appearance, one slab of concrete after another. However, everything came to a halt one day when a bulldozer unearthed what appeared to be human skeletal remains. Within the hour, two more skeletons were revealed. Foul play was suspected, and labor on the Interstate came to a temporary standstill.

The bureaucrats had to decide what to do next, and they had to reach their conclusion quickly. Freeway construction was already way behind schedule.

The mayor thought it logical that one of the congregations may have had a burial ground behind the church, but there were no records to support that theory. Finally, they reached the conclusion that the original owner of the house must have buried some family members there. At that time no one realized the owners had been a Madam and her so-called cousins.

Since the graves had already been desecrated, and nobody claimed to have any knowledge as to the identity of the bones, it was judged practical to continue with Interstate progress. The remains were reinterred in a cemetery about a mile away, and highway construction resumed as though nothing out of the ordinary had happened.

But something strange *had* happened.

On an overpass close to where the church had been, usually on foggy nights, faint apparitions materialized. Not just everyone noticed these manifestations. Truckers, overdue for a rest, observed them the most. At first they thought it was their imagination, and a few of them nearly ran their rigs off the highway due to the distraction.

~*~

I visited the truck stop again, determined to get to the bottom of the story. The ghosts of three different girls are seen periodically, dressed in clothing of the 1800's, or in undergarments identified with that time period: garters, corsets, mesh stockings and high laced-up boots, assumedly whatever each had been wearing at time of her burial.

Several men confessed that they had, at one time or another, taken the exit to help the woman. Was she in trouble? If not, maybe she would appreciate the companionship of a gentleman for the night.

Whatever she wanted, in each and every case, the attractive phantom-figure disappeared once the truck pulled to the shoulder of the highway.

"There's a puzzle piece missing," I told the bartender, as I sipped my Long Island Iced Tea. He finally took compassion on me and told me to talk to Chuck again. With a meaningful look, he said, "He's not told you everything there is to know." Then, he winked.

I went down the back hallway to call Chuck from a pay phone. I asked him if we could talk some more. He invited me to his place, and I remembered the officer who had said Chuck was harmless, so I went. I followed Chuck's directions and found the little ramshackle cabin he called home. It was well off the beaten path, near Horse Cave.

He was waiting for me, stationed on his front porch in a red Adirondack chair with a worn cushion. Barely recognizable, Chuck had a full set of teeth! He laughed when he saw my confused expression. "I only take my dentures out when I eat."

I nodded and said, "I see," but I was only being polite. I thought it should actually be the other way around.

He motioned me to make myself comfortable in an old

metal chair next to his. With a twinkle in his eye, he handed me a tattered, leather book and didn't say another word.

I had the feeling he'd waited a long time to show it to someone who would take it seriously. The first page was dated January 4, 1855, and had hand-written notations, entries like an appointment book:

Elwood Footstalker (morning)
Montrose Ederman (afternoon)

I skimmed the pages and realized this had been Madam's diary. My heart pounded, and I wondered how Chuck had come to be in possession of the journal. I didn't ask; I knew he would explain soon enough. I continued reading.

Madam's clientele came most often on Thursdays, Fridays and Saturdays, as steady and regular as clockwork. Dagwood Westerville was recorded every Sunday morning. I figured he must have snuck out of the house when his wife was away at church.

The Monday through Wednesday notes were cheerful ones:

May 2 — Eliza and Suzanne picnicked by the stream
June 6 — Leah and Charlotte hung laundry
— the others gathered herbs and firewood.

"Too bad the four day work-week didn't catch on," I said sarcastically. July 1 through 7 had been torn out of the journal. July 8 caught my attention:

July 8 — Dagwood, our Hero. Finished Leah's grave and we laid her to rest. Tied Elwood's feet and dragged his body with Dagwood's mare to the creek — threw his wretched corpse over the bank — evermore rid of our fears.

I glanced at Chuck, who, by that time, was chomping at the bit to finish the story himself.

"Dagwood Westerville was my grandpa," he volunteered.

Dagwood, I recalled, was the Sunday morning regular.

"He had a weekly fling with Madam," Chuck explained. "You see, Grandma had died giving birth to my mother, the youngest of three. Grandpa took the children to church every Sunday in his horse-drawn wagon, and he left them there with some church ladies while he went to the brothel."

I felt my eyebrows rise up an inch, my eyes were as wide as they could get, and I suppose my mouth had fallen open, because Chuck's next comment said it all:

"A man has *needs* after all, woman! Have a heart."

I swallowed and cleared my throat.

Chuck further justified, "The church ladies took the children home with their families after Sunday school and fed them a home-cooked meal. My mama told me they played with the other kids all afternoon, and Grandpa came in the early evening to retrieve them."

"Wow," I said, "the first recorded *play date* in history!"

Chuck nodded. "You could say that, I suppose."

I tapped on the book with my fingertips. "How did Leah die, and where are the missing pages?" I asked.

"Grandpa Dagwood destroyed them . . . but he told me all about it."

This I couldn't wait to hear.

"Saturday — seventh day of July — Elwood Footstalker had a romp with Leah. He'd been there Thursday and Friday, too, with Eliza and Charlotte, and he'd got awfully rough with them. The girls were scared of the man. Then, on

Saturday, he went plum berserk and strangled Leah." Chuck watched for my reaction.

I didn't even blink. "Go on," I said.

"Madam was beside herself, as you might imagine, and the girls insisted Elwood dig a grave. Madam planned to report the incident to the sheriff once Elwood was off her property. But, he must have heard them whispering behind his back, because he threw down the shovel, cussed and carried on, and said he'd call the sheriff himself and have Madam's illicit business shut down once and for all. Madam grabbed the shovel and gave Elwood a good smack on the head to shut him up. She didn't mean to kill him, but he died just the same."

"So . . . what happened then?"

"You read most of it. The grave was only halfway dug, but they laid Leah in it and covered her up with a quilt. They hid Elwood's body behind the outhouse and topped him off with compost. The next day, when Dagwood came to call, Madam ran out to his buggy, crying. He finished digging Leah's grave and hauled Elwood off to his eternal watery reward."

"Did Elwood's body ever surface?"

"Yeah, and when it did, nobody cared. Who'd give a hoot about somebody named Elwood Footstalker, anyway? Even to this day they say his ghost haunts one of the caves close by."

"Hmm . . . so, during Interstate construction was it Leah's grave they disturbed?"

"Damn straight! Hers and two of the other girls who'd died later on of natural causes. Dagwood dug their graves, too. It was a rugged life back in the mid-1800's don't you know? Those gals had rested in peace for over a century until their bodies were accidentlly unearthed and moved."

On my way home I pulled into the truck stop to chat with the bartender. "Thanks for the tip. You were right . . . Chuck cleared everything up for me."

He tipped his head and winked at me again.

I wondered if I could make him talk. I asked, "How did you know?"

"A bartender listens."

Fair enough, I thought. "Get this," I continued. "Some people say the spirits have returned to continue their careers, but others think the ladies seek Leah's revenge since they are known to appear only to men. What's your opinion?"

"Nah, not vengeance. None of the guys have been harmed when they pull off the road."

"True."

Then I thought about that one case I'd read about. At the police station I had found an intriguing accident report. A man had driven his Toyota into a guardrail last year, just past the overpass in question. His wife claimed that prior to the incident he had seemed suddenly distracted. She had demanded, "What are you looking at?"

His reply: "Nothing, dear."

Their Toyota was totaled, but the married couple survived with minor scratches.

Where There's Smoke

Near the end of the twentieth century, a small, wood-framed house in North Central Kentucky burned to the ground. To this day, it continues to smolder. Most people believe that the ghost of the man who died in the fire was cursed to smoke to all eternity. Several folks have described this phenomenon, each having their own version with varying details. I have researched, collected facts, and now attempt to reconstruct the story as closely as possible to the way it really happened.

Sandy Robinson had worked nights in the Maintenance Department at the University of Louisville for five years. He possessed a good work ethic and paid his bills in a timely manner. He didn't earn much money, and due to the remaining expenses from his parents' illnesses and deaths, there was little left over at the end of the week for socializing. He would have liked to go on a real date, or stop off for a beer with the guys once in a while. He didn't worry about his finances; he was young, and the University had a decent retirement plan. Sandy was frugal enough to save for a rainy day. He stashed five dollars cash each week in a coffee can on the bottom shelf of his old Frigidaire. *Cold cash,* he called it.

A rainy day came much sooner than he had expected, six months after he married his childhood sweetheart, Tonie

Maynard. In third grade at Minors Lane Elementary School, he had thought her to be the prettiest little brown-eyed girl he had ever seen, which is precisely when it struck him he'd like to spend eternity with her. But Tonie's parents divorced that year, and she moved to Tennessee with her mother. Sandy never forgot about Tonie, but didn't expect to see her again. To his amazement, when she returned to Louisville to attend college, she looked him up.

He was easily found, still living in his childhood home. By then, the faded yellow, two-bedroom house needed an extensive amount of repair. It had been Sandy's intention to fix it up, but most of his income had gone toward his parents' medical needs. They had died within thirty days of one another the previous year, and Sandy continued to make payments on the final hospital expenses.

Tonie had purposefully chosen to attend the Community College in Louisville; she hoped to find that cute little Sandy Robinson boy who had lived down the road, way back in her carefree days of childhood. But the street didn't look anything like she remembered; in fact, there was no real neighborhood left at all, so when she saw *Robinson* on the mailbox, she lifted her face heavenward and whispered *thank you*. She pushed the rickety gate open and all but skipped up the sidewalk. Praying Sandy hadn't gone and gotten himself hitched, Tonie knocked on the old front door.

They sat at the kitchen table, each with a tall, cold glass of sweetened tea, and Sandy explained how the area had changed so drastically. "My dad built this little house in 1948, and according to him, it was in the middle of nowhere. Through the years, it got smothered — subdivisions, trailer courts, strip malls — all haphazardly thrown into the mix. Then Interstate 65 came through and ripped three acres from us, putting our house a mere quarter-mile from the highway. Dad was a serious gambler, and after one season at Churchill Downs, the money we'd received for the land was gone."

"Oh, that's too bad," Tonie sighed.

"Yeah, and that's not the end of it. To make matters worse, UPS and the airport bought up much of the *surrounding* land. That pretty much robbed the family-friendly atmosphere from the vicinity. When the Gene Snyder Freeway sliced up our property, my folks had no choice but to sell most of it to the Highway Department. Finally, we were left with this half-acre here, trapped on a dead-end street. I tried to sell the house, but nobody wanted it, considering its location, location, location." Sandy gestured toward the kitchen window. "As you can see, the exit ramp comes to within 300 feet of the front porch!"

"Yes, I noticed," Tonie said sweetly, "but it's not like the house is on its last leg or anything. I mean, the inside, here, could be fixed up real nice."

"Sure, Tonie, and that's my plan, actually. Before he died, Dad would shake his head and talk nonstop about the old days. He'd insisted I invest the money we'd got from the latest land sale in a high-interest, long-term CD so he couldn't gamble it away! It'll mature next year, for which I'm grateful."

"See there, that's what I mean!" Tonie brightened. "There's still hope for this place after all." She looked the tiny kitchen over with a new perspective, envisioning modern, white cabinets with shiny brass knobs from H & S Hardware over on Preston Highway, and, at the window over the sink, red gingham curtains with white rickrack trim, custom made on her portable Kenmore sewing machine. Her redecorating plans didn't stop in the kitchen. As Sandy gave her a walking-tour of the house, she visualized the spare bedroom as a nursery for their first child. She saw a white baby crib, yellow ruffled curtains, and freshly painted off-white walls. She might even try her hand at stenciling; she'd seen some real cute Rubber Ducky patterns in a magazine.

Their courtship was short, sweet, and decisive. They wanted the same things out of life. They planned two children, and were pleased that their kids would attend the same school where they had met years ago. Tonie loved to read paperback romances while lounging in the swing on the front porch. She claimed it relaxed her, and she pretended the hum of Interstate traffic was actually that of the roaring surf. Although she had never been to the ocean, she knew what it sounded like. Sandy wondered what kind of life Tonie had in Nashville. Couldn't have been much if she was satisfied with her porch so close to the freeway. The only thing he ever caught a whiff of from its immediate proximity was exhaust fumes — certainly no ocean breeze!

Sandy returned from his shift one morning to find a stranger in his living room. The man wore prison-issue trousers and a black wife-beater shirt, exposing his muscular, tattoo-covered arms. He was sitting in Sandy's favorite chair as though he owned it.

"Hon," Tonie said, wringing her hands, "this is Rob Green, my half-brother. Rob was released on probation, and he just now showed up here on our doorstep."

"What were you in for?" asked Sandy.

"I was framed — three years for armed robbery and possession of Mary Jane." Rob smiled like a fox. He was missing two teeth — maybe three — from what Sandy could see. Sandy figured the teeth were causalities of prison fights.

Rob looked like he might have a short fuse.

Tonie had given Rob the spare bedroom, but he wouldn't stay long — only until he was back on his feet. Sandy wondered exactly how long *that* would take. He told Rob he was happy to meet him, which, of course, he really wasn't. He showered and went to bed. He lay there, listening to the whispered conversation between his wife and her brother. He searched his memory, unaware that a half-brother existed in Tonie's family. Her mother had remarried, so maybe the guy was in actuality her step-brother. Sandy sure as heck knew this wasn't anything he'd signed on for. He wondered if she had kept this information from him on purpose. Oh well, he thought, for better or worse. How bad could it be, anyway?

Later on, when Sandy awakened, he was appalled to smell cigarette smoke, and he knew right where it was coming from. He headed for Rob's room and tried to open the door, but it was locked. Sandy pounded on the door.

"Wadda ya want?" Rob yelled.

"Hey, man, don't smoke in the house . . . I'm severely allergic." This wasn't exactly true, but for sure he *was* allergic to death; Sandy didn't want to die of second-hand smoke. He coughed and faked a sneeze to make his point. Thirty minutes later he still smelled cigarette smoke coming from the spare bedroom.

Sandy left for work early that night, and he stopped by the Handy Food Mart where Tonie worked three evenings each week. Sandy told her he needed some straight answers from her. Tonie was stocking shelves, so she took her break, and they stood outside the rear door. As it turned out, Tonie's father had an affair several years before the divorce from her mother. The other woman, Hilda Green, had given birth to Rob during that time. After Tonie and her mother moved to Nashville, Hilda Green married Tonie's father, but she suddenly divorced him, walked away from both her husband and her son, never to be heard from again.

"I saw Rob on infrequent visits with my father," Tonie explained, "usually when I came to Kentucky for a week during the summertime. We were never close. In fact, he always frightened me somewhat, although I can't put my finger on any particular reason why. He's just creepy, is all."

"He's sinister, that's for sure, and he's smoking in our house. Do you think you can get him to understand the importance of not doing that? I told him, but the jerk has no respect for me!"

"I gotta get back to work. Don't worry, I'll see what I can do," Tonie promised.

Four weeks went by, and each morning when Sandy returned from work, Rob was sitting in Sandy's chair with an ashtray full of cigarette butts on the adjacent end table. The smell of old smoke permeated the place. Sandy imagined the drapes and furniture had soaked up plenty of it and would have to be shampooed once the moocher moved out. He might even have to reupholster his chair. Sandy had repeatedly reminded Rob of the smoking issue.

"Like I told you before, I only light up out on the front porch," Rob had claimed.

"Yeah, that's what you say. So, leave the ashtray out there, Bozo." *He's an idiot if he expects me to believe that,* thought Sandy. *That guy's on my last nerve.*

The final straw came on a Friday morning after work, when Sandy went to the Frigidaire to put a five-spot into the coffee can. His bank was empty! Rob explained that he had

needed the money for cigarettes and planned to replace it by tomorrow morning. *Rob the Robber,* thought Sandy, and he figured there must have been over three-hundred dollars in that can. He kicked himself for having left his rainy-day savings unprotected. He told the creep he'd give him one more week — then he'd have to move out. Rob shrugged, said, "No worries," and went into his room. He shut and locked the door and lit a cigarette.

Sandy took a shower and hit the sack for a few hours' shut-eye. Later that night, while shaving in the bathroom, he heard deep, muffled voices coming from Rob's room. Rob had a visitor, and Sandy was glad Tonie had stayed over at the Handy Mart to cover a co-worker's shift. Any friend of Rob's would definitely not be a friend of theirs, and he

73

would not have left her home alone.

At two o'clock the next morning, the Okolona Fire Department received a call. A traveler on Interstate 65 had seen smoke coming from a house near the exit. It turned out to be a three-alarm blaze. Okolona put a call for assistance into Fairdale, and another one to Brooks in the adjoining Bullitt County. The hydrants were located too far from the house, and the water pressure was weak. In the end, the dwelling was all but gone. The Fire Marshall reported that the fire had started in a mattress in the guest room, probably from a cigarette. Rob Green's corpse was barely recognizable; he was positively identified through his prison dental records.

The next day, after the investigators had completed their reports, Sandy and Tonie searched through the rubble. There were a few salvageable items, which they sadly collected and put in a cardboard box in the trunk of their car. The gray sky drizzled rain all morning, which made their task even more daunting. Sandy shuffled through debris on the old linoleum floor and stood in the skeleton of the kitchen. He thought about the day he and Tonie had sat at the Formica-topped table, drinking iced tea and making plans for their future. He pulled hard on the old Frigidaire handle, and when it opened, he was surprised to see everything inside looked good enough to eat. The stench warned him otherwise. He reached in for a package of sliced ham and a box of eggs. They were warm to the touch. He looked down at the coffee can, noticed the bulging plastic lid, and realized he would never get the money back from Rob now. He'd been saving for a rainy day, and today was as rainy as it got. Sentimental, he took the container out of the refrigerator to keep for old times' sake; he would start a new savings fund.

When he popped off the lid, to his amazement he found roll upon roll of twenty-dollar bills, wrapped with thick, red rubber bands. He counted the money, two-hundred thousand dollars in all. He called for Tonie, and they stared at one another for the longest time. They didn't say a word, just dropped the coffee can into the cardboard box with the rest of their reclaimed goods. They figured Rob must have had a drug deal last night, right under their noses in their own home, and put the booty in the fridge for safekeeping.

Their insurance adjuster put them up temporarily in a Holiday Inn; they ordered filet mignon from room service and the insurance company paid the entire bill. They took two weeks off from their jobs to settle their business matters and secretly felt they were on vacation.

Of course, Rob had no life insurance, so the family simply had him cremated without a funeral service. His father made it clear he didn't want his renegade son's ashes, so Sandy requested the crematorium place the remains in his old coffee can. Sandy Robinson had definite plans for Rob Green.

Sandy and Tonie had decided they didn't want to rebuild on the same piece of property, not only because of the location, but also due to the bad memories. The insurance company quickly settled their claim, paying them in full for the house and the land. On Tuesday of the second week, they went into Tri-City Olds and drove a brand new, baby blue Cutlass off the showroom floor and the next morning excitedly headed south on Interstate 65. Just before they crossed the Kentucky-Tennessee line, they took the Clark Road exit and stopped for breakfast at Dave's Bar and Grill. Afterward, they continued down the freeway to Nashville, where they took a few minutes to locate the house where

Tonie had grown up.

They sat in the car, looking at the house, and Sandy reached over for Tonie's hand. "So this is where the rest of your childhood happened," he said with a smile.

"No," Toni sighed. "I was never really a little girl here. My childhood ended when my parents divorced when I was ten."

Sandy squeezed her hand. He knew his parents had some rough times but had never considered divorce. He vowed to do everything in his power to keep his marriage to Tonie healthy and happy for the rest of their life together.

They drove off, and connected to Interstate-24 for a side trip to Chattanooga. After dinner at the Choo Choo Inn, they spent the night in an authentic passenger train car.

Thursday morning, they picked up a side road and headed back over to Interstate-65 and followed it all the way down to Mobile where they toured the *SS Alabama*. For dinner, they selected a restaurant across the street with a remarkable view of the battleship. They picked up Interstate-10 east, bypassed Pensacola, and went south on Highway 331 down to Seaside, Florida.

Tonie had seen the advertisement in a magazine. Seaside — a newly developed Gulf Coast community — the ideal place to raise a family. Sure enough, the instant they saw the quaint town, they knew they would never want to leave. Each home appeared to be painted with pastel watercolors, and the sand walkways cutting through the middles of the blocks enabled walking to the beach barefoot. They took their coffee-can cash, the insurance settlement, and the money from the matured CD and opened a bank account. They put a large down-payment on an emerald green, two-story cottage with a sunroom in the rear, and a front porch dripping with lots of white gingerbread trim. With the remainder of their money they would open their own Home and Pool Maintenance Company.

They drove back to Louisville, turned in their two-week notices, and loaded up their Oldsmobile with what little belongings they had left. They would buy new clothes and furniture on the Gulf Coast.

On his last night in Kentucky, after work, Sandy went to the fire site. The contractors had not yet cleaned up the disaster. He picked his way slowly through the remains of his old homestead, sprinkling two-thirds of Rob's ashes evenly around. He dumped the last third in the exact spot where Rob had died. He stood over the pile of ashes, head bowed, and said, "You wanna smoke? Go ahead and smoke, Chum. You can smolder throughout all eternity as far as I care." He turned and walked away, vowing never to return.

The next day they moved to Seaside. Tonie eventually sat on her second-floor balcony in a warm, Florida breeze, reading nursery rhymes to their two children, and in the foreground, the scent and sound of the surf relaxed her.

Back home in Kentucky, however, the events that followed weren't as relaxing. Not, at least, to the local firefighters. Nearly every Friday night, they received anxious calls from Interstate travelers — convinced they had caught a glimpse of smoke coming from a little house close to the exit ramp. The firefighters knew there were no buildings whatsoever at that location, and soon learned to expect these false alarms, but regulations dictated they respond to the calls just the same.

Morgan's Immortals

Fourth of July, 1970 — Greenville, Alabama. Totem poles in all shapes and sizes lined the walls of Dudley's Auction House. They stood alert with sad, watchful eyes, silently observing the sale of a lifetime on this scorching, summer afternoon. Restless and fidgety, the audience fanned themselves with their corrugated bid cards — carefully — so as not to submit an offer by accident.

Whack! The wooden gavel pounded the podium as the auctioneer shouted, "SOLD — to the pretty gal in the back!" Simultaneously, everyone turned in their seats to see who the winner might be.

Morgan Maefleur remained rigid, teetering on the edge of her chair. She had noticed the eyes of the totem poles staring at her, and now she detected a definite tremor of her hand as she held her card up high so Dudley could record her number. She was now the brand new owner of the century-old, two-story Stein-Bergen Building on the west side of the square in downtown Greenville.

Be careful what you wish for, thought Morgan. She had been selling vintage items at various flea markets on weekends and during summer vacation breaks — a hobby to subsidize her meager salary as a fourth-grade teacher. But Morgan had dreamed of owning her own bona fide antique shop, so at the age of fifty-three she retired from education and now quivered with excitement at the reality of it all. Would she be able to make a living this way? And what about the rumors that the structure was haunted? Morgan shrugged it off, figuring the legendary reports of ghost sightings had kept the cost low enough for her to afford it. She hoped if a ghost truly did inhabit the Stein-Bergen Building, it would be a friendly one.

The family had decided to sell the property after Hedrick Stein-Bergen's death at the ripe old age of ninety-eight. The street-level shop had been a marketplace for Hedrick, a renowned woodcarver, where he had peddled his totem poles and delicately whittled objects. On occasion, he had taken orders for customized poles, fashioned after the likeness of their future owners. He had permanently installed a whimsical pole replicating famous American Presidents in the front display window, which, in Morgan's opinion, would add to the ambiance of her own shop she would name *Morgan's Immortals.*

The large entryway was arched and meticulously trimmed out with two-tone bricks, an architectural style the narrow windows had duplicated, not only on the first floor, but on the second as well. The upstairs contained two apartments. One was a small studio which Morgan would call home and was accessible from a stairway in the shop. The other was a spacious apartment with a private entrance in the back. The large residence had been Hedrick Stein-Bergen's address for decades, and his estate had recently leased it to a young married couple with two cats. Morgan was happy to be an instant landlord, as she knew the rent payment would help pay her mortgage. She was counting on her retirement check and the income from her antique business to cover her other expenses, and she hoped to eventually earn enough money for another project she had on the back burner.

The day she moved her boxed goods and furniture into the shop was bright and sunny, like Morgan's mood. With the help of a local moving company, everything was delivered and in place by early afternoon. Morgan hung a sign on the front door to display her hours of business.

Morgan's Immortals
Open
Wednesday Thru Sunday 11-6.

She estimated it would take at least three days to set up, so she placed a *CLOSED* sign on top of the other one. Boxes sat two and three deep, all properly labeled. She dusted off an antique, oak pie safe, opened the boxes marked "holiday items" and hummed the tune of *Jingle Bells* as she arranged wooden gingerbread houses, Santas, snowmen and nutcrackers on the shelves. She kept the cupboard doors open and draped a green and red Christmas quilt over one and a red and white Five-Point Star quilt over the other. She strung a set of flickering red lights along the top and sides. She knew there was something to the *Christmas in July* theory and planned to be ready for it.

She barely noticed when a slender, young woman in a blue flowered dress, blonde hair precisely knotted just above the nape of her neck, walked purposefully through the entrance.

"Hello," the woman said cheerfully. "I'm Alice Stein-Bergen."

"Stein-Bergen?" questioned Morgan. She remembered seeing a similar-looking woman at the auction, but she recalled that lady had appeared much older. There was a definite family resemblance, however. "May I assume you were related to Hedrick?"

"Why, yes, of course, dear. He was my father. I stopped by to see if you needed anything."

"Well . . . um . . . thank you." Morgan thought surely the woman had meant to say *grandfather.* She smiled at her visitor, and noticed a basket Alice Stein-Bergen had carried in, covered with a blue and white gingham cloth. "Perhaps I *could* use a little break. Let me pull up a chair and we can sit and chat for a while."

The visitor deftly placed the tablecloth over a primitive folk art Shaker bench. She removed a Wedgewood tea pot and two sturdy china cups from her basket, placed each cup on a saucer, and tucked lace-trimmed napkins beside them. She opened a tin of shortbread cookies, dropped a sugar cube into each cup, and skillfully poured the steaming, amber liquid. Morgan watched, feeling quite helpless, but in a good way, like Alice in Wonderland at a delightful tea party, so entirely unexpected.

Alice Stein-Bergen sipped tea and gazed fondly around the old shop. "I *love* what you're doing with the place!" Happiness radiated in her voice and facial expressions as she spoke kindly of Hedrick and his fascination with wood-working. "I always enjoyed watching him carve and smelling the fresh timber." She inhaled deeply. "Most of his totem poles he carved from red cedar, you know."

The shop still had the leftover smell of cedar and sassafras. Morgan nodded. "The scent remains, doesn't it?" She imagined this place held delicious memories for Alice Stein-Bergen. Morgan thought, *Alice in Wonderland is sitting right here beside me!*

"He was thrilled when Interstate-65 was constructed so close to Greenville," Alice said, "because it brought an entire new group of tourists into the shop, and Hedrick loved to teach anyone who would listen to him. He'd go on and on with everything he knew about the history of poles."

"Oh, yes, I know. I taught fourth grade over in Montgomery, and I brought my class in here on a field trip a couple of years ago," Morgan explained. "He gave the kids such an amusing lecture that day."

Morgan glanced around the store at the built-in wooden wall shelves and remembered vividly. Her class had surrounded Hedrick at his workbench in the center of this shop while he explained the origin and concept of totem poles.

"Just because the tree has been felled doesn't mean it's not still alive," Hedrick had said. "It's taken another form, is all, and we can at least give it the vision to see where it's ended up at. That's why, no matter what I carve, I always give it eyes. That's my artistic signature — the eyes — and sometimes you have to look real hard to see 'em. They're not always where you think they'd be."

Alice added, "He was known for carving human faces on animal figures, and he'd put eyes in the back of their heads sometimes." Morgan had emptied her tea cup, and Alice refilled for both ladies.

"He spoke of the Great Spirit," Morgan said,

"so I inquired as to whether or not natives actually worshiped totem poles. He explained, that, no, but the stories they told often inspired admiration or reverence. The figures weren't gods or demons, but rather were symbolic, and each tribe had its own distinctive style."

"Uh-huh, that's true," Alice added enthusiastically, "and the poles tell stories or commemorate historical events. That's what he taught me." She bit off a piece of cookie and brushed the crumbs from her lap into her cupped palm.

"Yes, I remember that." Morgan said. "Their creation flourished in the 19th century, and they were painted in those early days using local materials. The class found that very interesting and asked lots of questions about how it was accomplished. Hedrick explained that white was obtained from clay, yellow from ochre, red from iron ore, blue from copper ore, and black from charcoal. Later, totem poles were colored using pigments and paints obtained by trading with the white settlers."

Morgan realized that she had been talking to Alice with the same tone of voice she would use to speak to a fourth-grader. She smiled at herself and thought, *You can take the school teacher out of the classroom, but. . . .* She removed another cookie from Alice's container. "I hadn't thought much about totems poles before that day." After a while she added, "It was heartbreaking to see them all being auctioned off."

"Totems were Father's life, and his life on earth is finished," Alice said, matter-of-factly. "And what a blessed life it was." She got up and prepared to leave. "You will undoubtedly find a few boxes in the very back of a built-in corner-cupboard by the restroom door. Whatever their contents, feel free to keep, or sell if you'd prefer. We've passed most of Father's small wood carvings down to family members." She took her exit through the front door as quickly and quietly as she had entered, leaving behind her blue checkered tablecloth.

Morgan, completely refreshed from the tea party, got back to her unpacking chores. In the rear of the store, she located the old cupboard Alice had described. Inside, were several medium-sized cardboard boxes. The first box contained two small, wooden antique trunks which Morgan estimated to be worth well over two-hundred dollars each. One was locked. She raised the lid on the second trunk and found a few screwdrivers, a hammer and some old, rusty nails. She scrounged through the hardware, but found no key to fit the other lock. Toward the bottom she saw a little bit of color. She dug deeper and uncovered a faded, toy soldier. Upon further examination, she realized it was a miniature nutcracker, about five inches tall. She stood the little fellow on top of the trunk and pushed its lever up and down, opening the soldier's mouth.

"Hello, pretty lady," Morgan said aloud in a deep voice.

"Why, hello, yourself! You're a handsome little man, and somewhat of a flirt, aren't you?" Morgan said. The nutcracker stared back at her through dark perceptive eyes. "Hedrick must have carved you — I can tell by your eyes. How awesome you are!"

She carried him up front to her Christmas cupboard and looked him over for some type of markings. Sure enough, on the bottom of his black boots, the piece was dated and signed H.S. She wondered why the family hadn't taken it to the auction. Hedrick's Totem poles were legendary and had sold for thousands of dollars that day. She put the nutcracker on a shelf beside a whimsical Santa, and while she secretly hoped no one would buy him, she placed a hand-printed sign next to him.

Nutcracker, Handmade
by Hedrick Stein-Bergen, 1940
$6,000.00

Morgan opened for business on Saturday. Her first customer was a man, dressed in a three-piece business suit, with two very unruly boys. He was interested in browsing more than buying, and didn't seem to notice his offspring playing hide-and-seek up and down the aisles. Morgan figured he must be divorced, and this was his every-other-weekend with his sons, for all the good it was doing them. She tried to keep her eye on the children, but other customers trickled in and out throughout the morning, and she lost track of what they were up to.

By closing time, she had sold only three primitive baskets and one McCoy vase. A large percentage of her customers had inquired of Hedrick, in hopes that Morgan might be selling some of the wooden sculptures for which he had been famous. She mentioned the nutcracker, but no one seemed interested in paying that kind of money for it. Morgan was glad; she had priced it high so she could keep it for herself. She would have to sell more than she had today, however, to stay in business.

Sunday morning, Morgan descended the stairs from her apartment to straighten up the display shelves in preparation for her second day of business. She sensed something out of place but didn't know what. Outside, she swept the front entranceway, taking a few steps back on the sidewalk to admire her window exhibit. She had placed a weathered metal, child's red wagon next to Hedrick's Presidential Pole, and filled it with vintage tin sand-buckets and shovels. Morgan had spread Alice's tablecloth out on the floor, topped with an old wicker basket filled with hard-plastic red plates and cups, a bottle of Chianti wine, and fake food items in the shape of French bread and Swiss cheese. Going for a beach theme, she had affixed vintage sunglasses upon the noses of the Totem presidents. An oversized glass vase filled with fresh wildflowers added to the display. Collectible stuffed bears sat on the floor, enjoying an Alabama summer picnic at the beach.

Morgan gave a start when she detected Hedrick's nutcracker in the wagon. She thought of the unruly boys from the day before and figured they had moved the little soldier. She headed for the Christmas Cupboard to place him back on his shelf, and wondered what other type of pranks those boys might have pulled when she wasn't looking.

Customers filtered in steadily throughout the day, but sales still weren't what Morgan had anticipated for her first weekend in business. People seemed more interested in Hedrick's absent figurines than in Morgan's Immortals.

Monday morning, Morgan was shocked to find the nutcracker missing from the Christmas Cupboard. He was back in the window display! "You're a little stinker, you are." Once again, she returned him to his shelf. "You really get around, I'll give you that." Morgan worried about herself, talking to a piece of wood like that, but the little guy's eyes were so realistic, she felt compelled to share her feelings with him.

Since she wasn't open for business on Monday or Tuesday, she finished unpacking, upstairs and down. The apartment tenants with the two cats stopped by to pay the rent, and browsed the shop for a while. By Tuesday night, Morgan was exhausted and ready to climb the stairs to her studio and call it a day. As she reached for the light switch by the back stairs, she glanced over at the Christmas Cupboard and realized that the nutcracker was missing yet again. *How can this be? There has been no one in here but me and my renters. Surely they didn't move him.*

Morgan cautiously walked to the front of the store, reached into the window display and picked up the nutcracker. *Someone is playing tricks on me. Perhaps it was the cats.*

Wednesday morning, it came as no surprise to Morgan when the nutcracker was, once more, in the front window. She held the little man in her hands, and gently moved his mouth up and down with the lever. She said in a low-pitched voice, "I like it in the window. I get to see everything going on out in the world. I feel lonely way back in the corner."

"Okay," Morgan said. "I'll leave you here, but you'll have to be content to stand on the floor with the bears because you look out of place in the wagon." She set him down and felt, more than heard, a little rattle coming from

the soldier. She examined him thoroughly. She realized that, with his mouth wide open, she could see a tiny switch inserted on the inside of his cheek. With a miniature screwdriver, she pushed on the switch. Immediately, the nutcracker opened in half, exposing a hidden cavity with a small key inside. *What on earth could this key unlock? I know — that antique trunk in the corner cupboard!*

Sure enough, as she inserted the key into the lock, the lid opened, revealing ten hand-carved wooden figures. *Exactly what my customers are asking for!* There were two little boys, a well-dressed gentleman, and several ladies all dressed to the nines. Each one had a similarity to the customers she had seen on her first day. *How odd.* She took the objects to her check-out counter, and placed a sign beside them.

Hedrick Stein-Bergen Figurines,
$200 ea.

By the end of the day, she had sold seven of Hedrick's carvings, two rare Wedding-Ring quilts, six vintage teddy bears, and a silver tea service. She thought perhaps she had underpriced the figurines, but still, her profit for the day was satisfying. She put the three remaining sculptures back into the little trunk for safekeeping. Tomorrow she would up the price on them to $400.

Thursday, much to her surprise, when she opened the trunk there were ten wood sculptures in it — the three from yesterday, and seven small Totem Pole statues, each with H.S. marked on the bottom. She priced the Totems at $500 each and they all sold by lunchtime.

Friday she opened the trunk to find the original three figures, along with seven more sculptures, three Totems and four figurines. Like before, the customers went wild over them.

The same thing happened on Saturday morning, and Morgan calculated that at this rate she would soon have made enough money to realize her other dream. She wanted to design and build a special classroom in her old school in Montgomery and set up a charity fund for children with learning disabilities.

Later that afternoon, the three-piece suited gentleman from the opening day came through the door, sans unruly boys. This is *his* every-other-weekend, for sure, Morgan thought. He seemed more relaxed than the previous Saturday, and wrote out a personal check for the three remaining figures and a six-hundred dollar set of Bakelite-handled serving utensils Morgan had paid $20 for at a tag sale the early part of June.

That same afternoon, the woman Morgan had seen at Dudley's Auction House entered the shop. She was much older, but the spitting image of Alice, and introduced herself as Hedrick's daughter, Annette. She inquired about business, was it good? Morgan felt compelled to tell her about finding, and selling, the original hand-carved figures. Annette seemed delighted with the news, and she browsed the store for a while.

Morgan was standing behind the cash register, when Annette hurriedly approached, frowning. She held out her hand, revealing Hedrick's nutcracker. "I wondered where this little guy had gone!" she said, breathlessly. "I looked everywhere for him. I was so afraid he'd been lost in the shuffle."

"Oh . . . well . . . he was in the trunk with the other wood carvings. Would you like to take him?" Morgan asked, holding her breath in hopes "no" would be the answer.

Annette caressed the nutcracker's face. "Father carved him from an old photograph of himself. It's a good likeness, actually. He really belongs right here in the store," she said softly, and stood him up on the counter. "My father was such a joy, and I miss him terribly." Annette sighed. "But, I'm content in that he had a wonderful, full life and such a great sense of humor."

"Yes, I catch a glimpse of wittiness in his fanciful carvings," Morgan replied.

"Oh, and not just that. He told some very humorous stories, too. Why, all the way up 'til he took his last breath, Father insisted that he and my sister, Alice, shared a tea party here in the shop each and every day!"

Morgan's brow furrowed. "What's funny about that? I had a tea party with her myself just the other day."

Annette looked suspiciously at Morgan. "Now that is just not possible, don't you see, because when my adventuresome twin sister was only nineteen years old she tried to tame a wild stallion! Unfortunately, the horse bucked her off and she died."

Morgan gasped and her eyes grew wide. "My goodness," she mumbled. "Is that where the ghost stories came from?"

"What, dear? Oh . . . those rumors . . . yes, I suppose so. Father and his vivid imagination." Annette reached once again for Hedrick's petite nutcracker and held it softly in the palms of her hands. "You want the icing on the cake?" She didn't wait for Morgan's response. "Father always told me that, when he died, his spirit would remain with this little man, so he could watch over his store for all eternity." Annette laughed, and she handed the nutcracker back to Morgan.

"Can you imagine such nonsense?"

Morgan nodded forcefully, and she glanced over at the tablecloth in the window display, where the nutcracker seemed most comfortable. "Yes, I can envision it quite well!"

On Sunday morning, Morgan set Hedrick in his favorite spot in the window, so he could see the world he had known and loved for 98 years. She revised the sign:

Nutcracker
Handmade by Hedrick Stein-Bergen,
1940
$6,000
Not For Sale

Haunted Indiana Dunes

At the northern terminus of Interstate 65, Dunes Highway takes off abruptly at a traffic light, bypasses Gary, and leads east to the Indiana Dunes State Park, founded in 1916. But long before the Interstate showed up, my parents toted me, our dog, a Coleman cooler, our family-sized tent and various camping essentials all the way from Indianapolis to the park for our annual family vacation.

A perpetual reservation for the first week of July — three adjoining campsites — accommodated everyone involved: aunts, uncles, and seven cousins, three of which were canine. Travelers from Illinois, Michigan, Wisconsin and a few other Hoosiers joined us in a large circle around our fire in the evenings, campers with whom we'd become friendly over the years. Darkness approached. Ghost story time was nigh. We shivered with delight.

My favorite was the one about the cadaver whose liver was stolen from the morgue and eaten by a totally disgusting, cannibal-type weirdo. At midnight, the dead guy showed up at the weirdo's house in search of his body part. He climbed slowly from the first floor, step-by-step (thirteen in all), to the second level, and by the time he got to number twelve I was spooked for good. "I'm on the top step. I want my liver back . . . BOO!" It got me every time. We girls giggled and squealed over the same stories, year after year.

One gloomy July we lost our desire to share ghost stories. The McMillan family, avid backpackers from Kalamazoo, was involved in a gruesome accident on their way to the Dunes, and the rest of us soberly accepted the news that they were lost to us forever.

Running alongside the Dunes Highway are two parallel railroad tracks. The family of three had waited twenty long minutes for an incredibly slow freight train to pass. As soon as the caboose went by, Mr. McMillan floored it, unaware of the speeding passenger train heading west toward Chicago on the second track. The couple probably never knew what hit them. Those were the days when seat belts and child seats were unheard of. Sherry McMillan, age five, was thrown from the car . . . a survivor, parentless evermore.

Two or three years later, now a teenager, I lost interest in vacationing with my parents. I reluctantly tagged along, however, though I left the storytelling adventures to the younger kids. The park consisted of over two-thousand acres of beautiful Hoosier landscape and included more than three miles of Lake Michigan's south shore, providing a magnificent beach and drifting sand hills distinctive to the dunes region. I joined the other teen girls, exploring the beach and its pavilion shelter at nighttime with a flashlight. During the day, we amused ourselves at the bathhouse and snack bar areas, positioned with attitude, striking our poses in skimpy bikinis for any cute boys who might happen by.

The residents of nearby Miller Beach reported that the evening sounds of the Dunes changed perceptibly after the McMillan tragedy. Vacationers agreed that they had never before noticed anything as eerie as the noises they now heard.

The winds seemed to blow just a little harder at night, and an audible whisper — shhhhheeeeerrrrrieee shhhhheeeeerrrrrieee — rustled through the dunes. One overzealous storyteller claimed Mr. and Mrs. McMillan returned each night in search of Sherry, calling her home to them. Everybody sitting around the fire nervously laughed it off at first, but with each passing night we finally had to agree that's exactly what it sounded like — shhhhheeeeerrrrrieee shhhhheeeeerrrrrieee — but was that really possible? There was no way to know for sure, but it did make for a good ghost story.

We had thought there was no way to know for sure until two years ago. The Gary Air Show, during Labor Day Weekend, featuring the Thunderbirds, Blue Angels, the Lima Lima Flight Team and others, had drawn a large crowd that Saturday.

About midday, one hundred yards out into the lake, came muffled pleas for help. Two women had been tossed into the rough water when their rubber raft was overturned by a large wave. They flailed and bounced around in what appeared to be a strong undertow while the sightseers on the beach yelled for help.

A middle-aged resident of Miller Beach had been relaxing on his deck and heard the commotion. He had been a swim instructor in college, and although he hadn't used his skill for many years, he attempted a rescue.

He grabbed a life jacket from an unattended lifeguard station and headed out swiftly. He tossed the jacket to the gal who seemed to be struggling the least, watching as she slipped it over her head. He assumed she would grasp the life jacket and hang on. He took hold of the second lady and towed her to shore, watching the other girl as best he could. She seemed to be following him okay at first, but suddenly he realized she was no longer in his line of vision.

He got the first lady to shore and left her there for others to care for her needs. He swam back to the approximate location he had last seen the other woman, but he never found her. The life jacket washed up on shore about a quarter-mile away later that afternoon, the straps torn partially off.

The rescued woman was hospitalized and suffered a temporary memory loss due to the shock of the event. For the remainder of the weekend, spectators assumed that a wickedly strong current had torn what must have been an already weakened belt from the life jacket, and it had no doubt slipped off of the other unfortunate lady.

On Monday morning, however, the facts became known to all. The woman who vanished was found by a local fisherman, and her identity was quickly verified. Sherry McMillan from Kalamazoo, Michigan.

Since that day, not once has anyone, neither resident nor camper, heard those rustling sounds of shhhhheeeeerrrrrieee shhhhheeeeerrrrrieee at night in the Indiana Dunes State Park. And why should they? Sherry's parents had been calling her home for years. She had joined them at last.

The Moving Mansion

Athens, Alabama — 1953

Elmer Joseph Boonswallow's death occurred early on a frosty January morning. In his colossal suite on the third floor of Boonswallow Manor, his antique English canopy bed was encircled by a doctor, three nursemaids in crisp white uniforms, and a horde of family members. Freshly pressed handkerchiefs dabbed eyes; sobs and moans echoed down the corridor and around the corner into the adjacent sector of the stately mansion.

If the house servants had been tucked into their assigned spaces, they would have easily heard the commotion from their quarters, one floor below. But they were attentive, on-call at the entrance area of their master's domain, tending to the family's many needs — *a shawl for my wife, quickly now! Earl Grey with lemon (and make it hotter than the last pot); an upholstered chair (this one is much too uncomfortable); tend that fire (Boy, can't you feel the chill in this room?)*. On and on they whined.

Elmer Joseph, AKA Elmo Joe, was not surrounded by loved ones because he was a loved man. Not by a long shot.

Where there's a will, there's family, and Elmo Joe's Last Will & Testament, concealed in a locked box, was to be read within minutes of his death by his legal representative.

The lawyer, Wilbur Mayberry, was a wiry fellow with gray whiskers and a handlebar mustache. He hovered in one corner of the room, fidgeting with a key in the left pocket of his pinstripe pants.

Elmo Joe lived to the age of 103. He had lingered during the last two years, precariously teetering on the edge. His death had taken way too long; the final family scene had been reenacted four times already. His great-nephews wondered if he would ever die at all.

Everyone muttered and sniveled with relief. The moment they had waited for had arrived. Each person in the room expected to get a piece of Elmo Joe. And why shouldn't they? He had enough pieces to go around two or three times. They would all be rich and — the very best part — rid of Elmo Joe forever. That's what they thought.

Elmo Joe was born in 1850 to wealthy parents. Twenty years later they surprised him with a baby sister. (His parents were considerably stunned, as well.) He called her Sister.

Through the years, Porter, his brother-in-law, had squandered Sister's inheritance, which was not surprising to Elmo Joe. He had always suspected the man to be more interested in Sister's financial value than her happiness. What little savings Porter and Sister had left vanished on Black Tuesday, October 29, 1929.

Elmo Joe had invested his share of the family money wisely and prospered during even the worst of the Great Depression in 1933, shaking his head at the young whippersnappers who didn't. He loaned Porter and Sister enough to help them get back on their feet, but at an exorbitant rate of interest. They, in turn, loaned some of the money to their own children and grandchildren at a higher percentage, which allowed them to make their own timely payments. *Timely payments, timely payments* — notorious phrasing in all of Elmo Joe's business contracts.

Elmo Joe owned two high-rise apartment buildings in Huntsville, and though he wasn't a slumlord, he was known for being slow in the maintenance department. On occasion, the elevator would not work (not a good thing for the elderly living on the higher floors), and he switched over to a boiler heating system the first day of September, eliminating the ability to use air-conditioning, even though temperatures in early fall were routinely over seventy-five degrees.

He was a demanding landlord and insisted his tenants follow his distinct Rules of Apartment Living — or else. He would not allow the walls to be painted any color other than white; this applied also to ceilings, of course. He allowed no frying of fish (it stunk up the entire building), no smoking indoors, no loud music, and definitely no pets of any kind, not even an old lady's yellow canary. Upon routine inspection, he had found one in a widow's studio unit on the fifteenth floor and immediately evicted her (after he opened the cage door, dispatching the bird out the open window — never to be seen again).

Elmo Joe rented to his nephews and nieces at a discount — five percent—but only if they paid one month in advance. If their payment was overdue, he demanded the cumulative discount he had allowed them for the entire period of their past lease. If they were unable to come up with the money in seven days, he moved them out despite their pleadings — set them right out on the sidewalk — like any other negligent tenant.

One day, Elmo Joe had wondered if God felt the same

satisfaction as he did when He was called upon to punish irresponsible people. But he was a non-religious man, and later that same day he remembered that he had previously come to the educated conclusion that God does not exist.

When Elmo Joe pulled their strings, both family and business acquaintances danced like marionettes. They endured his eccentricities and jumped through his nonsensical hoops for the financial advantages it provided them.

Wilbur Mayberry read the will aloud in the library. Everyone in the audience sat straight in their chairs, eager with anticipation.

> The estate's assets were listed as follows:
> Two luxury high-rise buildings
> An innumerable amount of stocks and bearer
> bonds worth millions
> A Savings and Loan office in Florence
> A prosperous Ford dealership in Decatur
> Half-ownership in a new steak and pancake
> enterprise (whose franchises were selling like
> . . . well, hotcakes).

Porter and Sister, now in their early eighties, delightedly added numbers in their heads. They figured they would inherit the most. They would travel the world — first class, of course.

Only those present in the room at Elmo Joe's death were to be beneficiaries. Anyone else was out in the cold. (Mayberry's secretary had leaked that fact as rumor, which explains why the bedroom suite had been filled to capacity that day.)

Other than the mansion, all assets were to be sold and placed in a fund, aptly called Boonswallow Manor Trust, to provide for maintenance and repair.

The heirs — the doctor, nurses, lawyer, family members and servants alike — shared the benefits of Boonswallow Manor Trust equally. But there was a catch. To claim the inheritance, they were required to live together in the mansion. The trust would generate a hefty monthly allowance for each family member unless they chose to move out of the house.

Elmo Joe's Rules of Apartment Living applied here, too. The walls could not be painted any color but white, no fish frying, no smoking, no loud music, no pets, and so forth.

Once the initial shock wore off, cries and moans of horror emanated throughout the manor.

The great-nephews and nieces tried to comfort their parents and grandparents. They pointed out that they had lived by these rules previously — these conditions were nothing new — but the older crowd was inconsolable. Their agitation was caused by the fact that they had to share their windfall with the lawyer, the doctor, the nurses and the servants, each of whom was to receive a generous annual stipend.

Wilber Mayberry curiously watched the pandemonium. He recalled Elmo Joe's obnoxious laugh the day he signed his will. *How disgusting that he can control people from the grave,* he thought. Mayberry had moved into the mansion two weeks ago and planned to remain, although it troubled him to think he would have to live in the close vicinity of the others. He looked forward to semi-retirement, and he planned to pursue his favorite pastime — fishing in Wheeler Lake near Muscle Shoals. He knew he couldn't fry fish in the house, but grilling them on his campsite would suffice, a small price to pay for the luxuries he was about to enjoy. He couldn't believe his luck and was one of the few present who actually appreciated what Elmo Joe had given him.

Mayberry patiently waited for the bedlam to calm down before he read the final request of Elmer Joseph Boonswallow:

> *My corpse shall be embalmed, interred in a customized gold coffin, sealed in a vault that has been constructed in the cellar of Boonswallow Manor.*
> *The Manor will never be sold or demolished.*

If it is sold or demolished, said estate recipients will forfeit all future inheritance. In that instance, the remaining funds in Boonswallow Manor Trust will be distributed to the United States Government to use as it sees fit.

All twenty-six bedrooms of the manor were occupied by the heirs, and eventually most of them learned to get along. Some quickly found the Rules of Apartment Living tedious, however.

Sister grew tired of her bedroom's white walls, for she was a colorful woman who had always preferred jewel-toned

decorating. She hired a painter; the east wall he painted sunshine yellow, the west wall royal purple, the north wall brilliant red, and the south wall jungle green. Sister was delighted with the results and tipped him generously.

The next morning when she awakened she opened her eyes and shrieked in terror. Her great-grandchildren ran down the hall and into her room to see what her problem might be.

All the walls were white, as though they had never been painted! Sister demanded her money back from the painter, but he refused.

One of the nurses had a Siamese cat and was determined to move it into the mansion with her. She kept it secreted away, but soon it went missing. She looked in every nook and cranny, anywhere a cat might find a hiding place, but the feline was never found.

The doctor had kept his smoking habit a secret from everyone. He felt it was a shame that a man who took care of others' health would do something so careless to his own. The day he moved in, he unpacked three cartons of Winston cigarettes, and hid them in a drawer with a secret bottom. The next morning, he slid the bottom of the drawer open, only to find it empty.

Wilber Mayberry was the last one to deviate. He had taken a long-awaited fishing trip to Oregon, and he returned with a large catch of salmon. He spent one afternoon in the sizeable kitchen, prepared various vegetable side dishes, rubbed an herbal mixture on the salmon and baked it in the commercial-style wall oven. He was joined in the dining room that evening by the other household members who consumed the gourmet feast with delight.

The next morning, the kitchen was locked, the deadbolt shut from inside. Seven days later, remarkably, the lock came open, just as curiously as it had been bolted the week before. They had apparently suffered a loss of power in the kitchen. Servants tossed out bags of spoiled food and completely cleaned and sanitized the refrigerator.

"Great-uncle Elmo's ghost inhabits this house," voiced a relative. "The Rules have been ignored!"

"But the salmon was baked, not fried," the doctor said.

"The odor is still a fishy one," a servant added.

"Perhaps it's simply better not to toy with the Rules," said the doctor.

The heirs held a household meeting and decided to strictly abide by the Rules of Apartment Living rather than create any further madness. For the next eight years, no one ever ventured down to the cellar, for the one thing they all agreed upon was that Elmo Joe's ghost definitely inhabited it.

Then, something entirely unexpected happened. The Highway Department was bringing Interstate 65 through, purchasing land, tearing down houses. The plans called for the freeway to cut right through the middle of Boonswallow Manor.

Mayberry battled with a number of stubborn officials to get them to understand fully the complexity of the situation. The Last Will and Testament had specifically stated the manor could not be demolished for any reason. Everyone would move, lose their liberal monthly incomes, and worse yet — the remaining millions of dollars held in trust would be handed over to the United States Government. That outlook was particularly distasteful to residents, but the officials insisted they had to get the structure out of highway's path, one way or another.

Which gave Mayberry an idea — *move* Boonswallow Manor!

It took a serious amount of palm-greasing for the Highway Department to reach an agreement with the estate recipients. The house would be transported nine-hundred feet to the west and settled on a fine, six-acre section of prime land.

The lawyer called a household meeting. The heirs had only one question. What about the cellar?

"It will be filled in immediately upon the removal of the manor," Mayberry explained. "The Highway Department offered to pour a new cellar if we so desire."

Wide-eyed, everyone's thoughts went downward to Elmo Joe's solid gold coffin, and, without another word, they boarded up the walls of the cellar, hiding all evidence of the vault's existence.

The manor was moved without incident, the cellar filled with concrete.

Boonswallow Manor has changed for the better. Sister spends summers traveling throughout Europe with her granddaughters. When in Alabama, she enjoys vibrant, colorful walls in her boudoir.

The doctor bought a burgundy, silk smoking-jacket and rolls his own smokes with a custom blend of tobacco.

Rock and roll forcefully echoes from the rooms of the youth.

The cat-loving nurse has Butters, a female Siamese, and a lady Persian named Picnic. She is considering an Abyssinian male which she will call Encore.

Wilber Mayberry is an avid angler at Wheeler Lake. He fries trout and smallmouth bass in the manor's kitchen, and complements his meals with a variety of the other residents' favorites: cheese grits, fried apples, hush-puppies, sliced tomatoes, fried okra and iced tea. The entire household joins him in the stately dining room every Monday night. They occasionally package up their leftovers for donation to a homeless shelter in Huntsville.

Trucks and automobiles on the Interstate drive right over a solid gold coffin, ten feet below, but Elmo Joe's ghost is trapped inside and there is not one thing he can do about it.

We hope.

Oliver T.'s Story

I'd be nearly ninety years old by now if I hadn't died so young. My great-grandpappy lived to be ninety-nine, and I always planned to live at least that long. Alas, it was not meant to be.

Ah, well, I suppose it all turned out okay in the end.

In these modern times, enlightened people claim that a spirit can choose not only the timing of his entrance as a physical being, but his exit as well. Back when I took my departure, though, we weren't as free-thinking, although I suspect my young daughter, Olivia, had a sixth sense about these matters. She was the most open-minded kid I'd ever known. Olivia was not frightened by my death. She accepted it with grace and maintained a remarkable mood of calm, especially for a twelve-year-old. For that I was grateful, because heaven knows her mother sure needed someone she could lean on. I did all I could, but Olivia's gift of intuition helped Evelyn out more than anything.

They say your life passes before your eyes when you die. It's true — that's the way it happened to me. At first I thought I was dreaming, and maybe I was. But somewhere along the line there was a transition of sorts.

I never saw a bright light like some folks claim. Maybe that's because I was nowhere near ready to go. And why *should* I have been ready? I was only forty-one years old! But you're probably more interested in the memory flash than the bright light.

There I was, just a little kid, following behind my daddy while he plowed the fresh earth on our farm in Franklin, Indiana. My brother, Wesley, was two years younger but just as eager to help. We played each night until after dark, chasing fireflies. Oh, what blessed times those were. Funny, I had not thought of my days of childhood for years, and, even though I knew I was dying, the remembrance made me happy.

In school, I sat next to Evelyn Montgomery, and we passed silly notes back and forth. I sometimes wondered why she kept her bangs cut so short. She'd have looked better if she'd let them grow out long like the rest of her hair. But, who cared? I didn't think of her as anything but a neighbor girl, just another classmate.

Then came my sixteenth birthday.

I'd been born on a Christmas Day, so, just before winter break, Evelyn gave me a jar of jam she'd made from the grapes in her father's arbor. She had it wrapped up all fancy with brown tissue, and a bow of red and green ribbon was wrapped around the top. *Happy Birthday, Oliver T.* was delicately printed out on the brown wrapper — I think she'd addressed it to me before she packaged it.

I discarded the tissue and ribbons and put the container on the kitchen table after school. Mama picked it up, looked it over and raised one eyebrow. She offered me one of those *I know something you don't know* smiles that she was famous for.

I held my hands out to my side, palms up, and shrugged.

I sauntered into my room and threw my books onto the floor, kicked 'em under the bed, glad to be rid of them for two whole weeks.

Mama baked hot biscuits the next morning, the jam jar placed next to my plate. I crammed one biscuit after another into my mouth — this was the best stuff I'd ever eaten.

"Why, Oliver T. Winston, that Montgomery girl's sweet on you," Mama said, her pointy finger touching the tip of my nose. "The way to a man's heart is through his stomach, don't ya know?"

No, how would I have known that?

Now she tells me, I thought. I retrieved the wrappings from the waste bin, folded them neatly and placed them in the top drawer of my bureau. I wondered how I could possibly wait two more weeks to see Evelyn again.

I went back to school in January with a fresh awareness. I followed that girl around everywhere, since she'd picked me for her beau and all. At first she acted like I was a nuisance, and I wondered if I had misunderstood her intention, but later on I heard a song that said a boy chases a girl until she catches him, and everything made perfect sense after that. So that's pretty much what happened with me and Evelyn.

We'd been married only a few months when I was

shipped out for WWII. My brother was in the Navy same time as me, and once, with my ship docked at Pearl Harbor for two weeks R&R, I checked the list of soldiers to see if there was anyone I knew there. Lo and behold, whose name did I find on it but Wesley's? Those two weeks held a lot of recollections for me — the newspaper at home even ran a story on us with our pictures on the front page. That experience was especially vibrant in my *everything flashing before my eyes* adventure.

We chugged beer, chain-smoked our Chesterfields and spent quality time with a couple of pretty gals. Now, don't go thinkin' I was unfaithful to Evelyn. I just enjoyed the *companionship* of the girls — it's good having a female who smells of lavender to talk to when you've been on a ship with a hundred grease-monkeys for eight months! Sure, the girls probably expected more from us, and one of them mighta got lucky, I don't know for sure. I can't vouch for Wesley's behavior, but then, he was single at the time.

My memories flashed forward to Olivia's birth. Holding that little bundle in my arms, the strong feeling of fierce protection I felt for her—well, it was the most amazing emotion I'd ever experienced. I promised her on the day she was born I'd always be there to look after her. So how could I leave her when she was only twelve years old?

That's just the thing — I couldn't!

I'd known I wasn't well. I had tried to quit smoking, and I cut way back on the beer. I'd decided to make a doctor's appointment, but I was working overtime and hadn't the energy as of yet. Back then, we didn't know anything about high cholesterol. I had a daily fat intake that clogged up my arteries, and I died before I knew what was going on.

Myocardial infarction, they called it.

I had an hour before I left for work, so I reclined in my chair for a short nap. I floated upward, had the memory flash, watching everything from a vantage point close to the ceiling. I heard Olivia's school bus, and she clamored around in the kitchen for a bit. I knew she'd come in and find me dead, but there wasn't a single, solitary thing I could do about it.

Odd it was, that point in time. Olivia came and knelt beside me. She took my hand, and frowned. Then she looked upward and spoke to me. "I know you'll always be here for me, Daddy." She ran into the kitchen and called the police. It was too late, but she'd hoped for the best, I suppose.

I'd made my promise to her, so I stuck to my word. I hung around pretty much all of the time for the first couple of years. Olivia even set a place for me at the table, while Evelyn clucked and wagged her head, but my little girl was undaunted. I was so proud of her. I joined them and listened in on their conversations. Evelyn hated her job and she spouted off every evening about one person or another she worked with who wasn't carrying their load. Seemed Evelyn had to do everyone's chores plus her own. Olivia advised her to quit covering for people, so the boss would find out, and they'd get fired. Evelyn never listened to Olivia.

Olivia married her high school sweetheart, Bud, and though I can't say he would've been my first choice, he turned out to be okay after all. Shows what an over-protective father knows. I think dads in the flesh have that problem — they never approve of their daughter's boyfriend. So why would I be any different? She wouldn't listen to a solid daddy, so why should a transparent one expect to be heard where love is concerned?

My preference for their first home was that Bud (*Bud — what kind of a name is that?*) should have moved her into a little rental down the road, but he bought her a used, pink trailer, of all things. Oddly enough, Olivia seemed to be thrilled with it and turned it into a romantic cottage, pink calico at the windows, pink plaid in the rugs, and pink gingham check on the bedspread. She mimicked the theme from the sink, stove and refrigerator, which was entirely old-school, as copper-tone was the *in* shade for kitchen appliances at the time.

Apparently, Olivia was smarter than I gave her credit for, because Bud quickly felt just a tad overwhelmed by all the pink in his home. Within a couple of years, he'd built a large, log house — *a man's house*, he'd called it. She decorated it with blue and green plaids and stripes, no calicos or flowers anywhere in the fabrics, and her hubby's been a happy man ever since. Even now, though, I see him look at old photographs of the little trailer, and he'll sit, alone, and study them, remembering the good times they had in those early days.

They had two sets of twin girls, and eventually Bud gave up trying to fit the description of a man's man, whatever that is. When his girls were teenagers, they labeled him *retro-male*. He just shook his head and smiled. Ha! I wish I could've known him in person, gone fishing and to ballgames with him. We would've had great times together, Bud and me.

Evelyn went through a bout with cancer, and for a while there I thought she might join me. But she went into remission and was finally pronounced cured. What a difficult time that was for the entire family. I'd been instructed that, if I hovered too close, Evelyn might be enticed to just throw in the towel and not fight for her earthly life as hard as she should. I tried not to hover, but I had to be there for Olivia. I would've loved for Evelyn to join me, but I didn't want my daughter to lose another parent.

By then, everyone called my wife *MeMaw*, but she'll always be Evelyn to me.

Bud remodeled their walk-out basement into an apartment, so Evelyn had herself a mighty nice mother-in-law pad. Good thing for that, because the Highway Department had bought up our old property to build another on/off ramp. They leased a portion of our old land to Evelyn, so she could pursue a dream we'd always had: a diner where you could get breakfast twenty-four hours a day.

In retrospect, I think those breakfasts were what killed me, though, what with all that fat from the bacon and the generous portions of butter I'd topped her biscuits off with. Plus, she used lard to make those biscuits and fried them in lard, too, and well, yeah, I'm pretty sure that's what did me in. Truth be told, I should've had those heavy breakfasts only on weekends, and eaten lighter the other five days. Hindsight's 20-20, so they say. Nowadays they'd easily do bypass surgery and I'd be good to go for thirty more years, at least. In any case, Evelyn changed to healthy cooking styles, and her diner was a blazing success.

My four granddaughters own *MeMaw's Breakfast Anytime* now. Evelyn got herself hitched to a traveling salesman named Nelson Milligan from Ft. Lauderdale, and they're living out their retirement years playing tennis in a ritzy club with clay courts and walking the beach barefooted with their little Westchester Terrier, Fuzz Ball.

I searched for over a year to find a proper second

husband for Evelyn. She claimed to be content as a widow, but I knew better. I couldn't cross over for good and leave her like that. I knew she'd be happier if she had someone her own age to settle with. By then, she knew I was lingering because my image had shown up on some photographs, so I couldn't just go off and leave her alone. Once I'd made the decision to direct Nelson Milligan's path, everything fell into place. He caught on real quick to my scheme and went right along with it.

I've met a spirit with whom I've become particularly close, and we've decided to reincarnate in physical bodies so we can be even closer, if you know what I mean. We've selected two sets of parents and need to wrap up a few loose ends, and then we'll be on our way.

Yes, I've had a good life . . . the one down below, the one in the middle, and the one above. You see, I can go back and forth as often as I please. You think you'll have lots of questions when you get to heaven? Yeah, that's what people believe. And there *are* answers here, don't get me wrong, but not necessarily the ones you might want.

If you wonder why I don't wait for Evelyn, it's because you can't reincarnate in the same family position with the same person. I had the opportunity to come back as her grandson when Olivia was pregnant. But we had these girls up here who insisted on being twins. We drew straws. I lost. I can never be Evelyn's husband again, not in the way I was.

My lady friend and I are coming into families who currently live in a quaint neighborhood in Ft. Lauderdale. Another twenty years, we'll marry, and by then Evelyn will have been in the spirit world for a while. (She's going to die peacefully next year in her sleep. Don't worry — she'll be fine.)

You remember those silly notes we passed back and forth in school? You might not believe this, but trust me when I say: up here there's a message board. So I've left her a note and told her it'd be an honor if she chose to come back as my daughter someday. I hope she does, but the decision is hers. Yes, it's true; we *can* choose when we're born. The departure, however, well . . . I'll leave that up to you to find out once you're here. I've always been a kind spirit, unlike some I've known. I would never want to ruin the ending for you.

(See *Proof On Film* and *MeMaw's Breakfast Anytime*)

The Persistent Organist

It was going to be a White Christmas, and I was anxious to get off the road, back home to a cozy fire. I stopped at a rest area near White House, Tennessee on Interstate 65 to stretch a bit. I washed my hands and reached for a towel, when sounds of Vivaldi filled the air. I glanced at the ceiling and saw a loudspeaker, but the music seemed to be coming from all around.

I hummed along — the allegro movement of Concerto in F, one of my favorites — and although the piece was written for violin, organ and strings, in this case a solo organ accomplished the work beautifully. I felt the vibrations from my head to my toes. If someone had told me a pipe organ was located just outside the ladies room window, I would have believed them.

A hefty, red-headed woman wearing a pink cotton maintenance department uniform, *Dainie* embroidered on her pocket, mopped the floor at one end of the large restroom.

"Merry Christmas," I said, as I headed for the door.

"Same to you, Lassie. Are ya ready for it?"

"No," I snorted. "I always wait 'til the last minute."

"Aw, well. I finished wrappin' my last present Saturday," she said.

"If only *I* were so efficient. Maybe this Vivaldi Christmas music will put me in the mood. I've never heard such a wonderful sound system in a rest stop anywhere else along the Interstate. I absolutely love the pipe organ."

"Oh, really, do ya, now?"

Right about then, the music came to a halt, and a scratchy elevator tune barely dribbled from the speaker.

I found my way through the light snow back to my Saturn. Suddenly, *The Hallelujah Chorus* blurted out from the heavens.

I looked at the outside of the building, but there were no speakers installed. *Could it be coming from someone's vehicle?* I checked to see: none of the cars parked alongside mine were occupied.

I felt compelled to walk around the main building, and I discovered that the melody originated from a metal storage shed in an overgrown field behind it. An eerie feeling came over me. I went back inside and located Dainie, the cleaning lady.

She smiled knowingly, as though she expected me.

"What's up with the organ music?" I asked.

"Hah! That's the same question I asked myself many years back," Dainie said.

"Hmm." I paused, but she said nothing more. "So," I ventured, "*is* there an answer to that question?"

"Depends on if you believe in ghosts or not. If ya do, then, yes. If ya don't, well…I'm not gonna waste my time." She stood her mop up on end and glared at me.

"I didn't believe in ghosts before, but now, since traveling this interstate, I'm a believer."

"Guess you've never been 'round this way on a Sunday mornin', 'cause you would've heard it if you had. First time for me was when I hired on here. Back then, I was doin' same as now, mopping. All of a sudden, *The Wedding March* blared out of nowhere."

"Oh I love that one, too, *The Wedding March From A Midsummer Night's Dream* by Mendelssohn," I said. "What must you have thought?"

"Honest to God, Missy, it sounded just like a church organist I knew as a kid. I was here alone, and I was terrified."

"Why?"

"Cause she'd been dead for years! It was her, though, doing the playin'. The old organ she used to play is piled up in pieces in that little shed behind this place."

I turned that tidbit over in my mind. "So, do you think the music is supernatural somehow?"

"I don't think it, Missy; I *know* it. The ole gal's ghost performed for nearly an hour that day. By the time she'd finished, she'd done *Arrival of the Queen of Sheba* by Bach; *Behold the King;* and *A Mighty Fortress Is Our God.* 'Course I didn't know the names of the songs back then, but I've heard 'em over and over throughout the years, so I've learned a little somethin' about titles and composers.

I asked Dainie to tell me all she could about the mystical musician.

"She was Magda Maude Mandenheim, one of the foremost organists of the early twentieth century. She was born in 1870 in Erlangen, Germany, near Nuremburg and immigrated with her parents in 1880. Their name is registered in a big book on Ellis Island," Dainie said.

"How well did you know her when you were a child?" I asked.

"Not nearly as good as I know her now. Years ago, she was the organist at a church I went to down the road from here. My mother was best friends with her," Dainie explained. "Soon as I first heard the music, I went straight off to the old-folks home where Mother lived. She had asked for a keepsake after Magda Maude passed, so the family gave her the woman's childhood diary. I'd seen it before, so I was anxious to read it again. That diary told me a whole lot about little Magda Maude. She was so fascinating; somebody should write a book about her."

I shared with Dainie that I was a writer and explained my interest in ghost stories.

"I sensed that about you somehow," she said. Without another word, she led me down a hallway into a large supply closet. She worked a combination lock and opened the gray, metal door of her personal storage locker. A leather-bound journal lay on the top shelf.

"I keep it here so I can read parts of it once in a while. You sit here on this bench and study it if you want. I'll finish up in the ladies room and be back in a little while."

Magda Maude Manndenheim's penmanship was elaborate, so typical of the 1800's style of scripting. She did not make daily entries, thus the journal consisted of several years of Magda's history.

She described her family's voyage to America and their new home in New York in Upper Manhattan:

> *I will love it here in America in spite of the fact that the Americans changed our last name to Mann at Ellis Island. My new schoolmates call me Manhattan Mag-Mann. Father and Mother say it makes no difference what one's name is — children always make fun of newcomers and foreigners.*

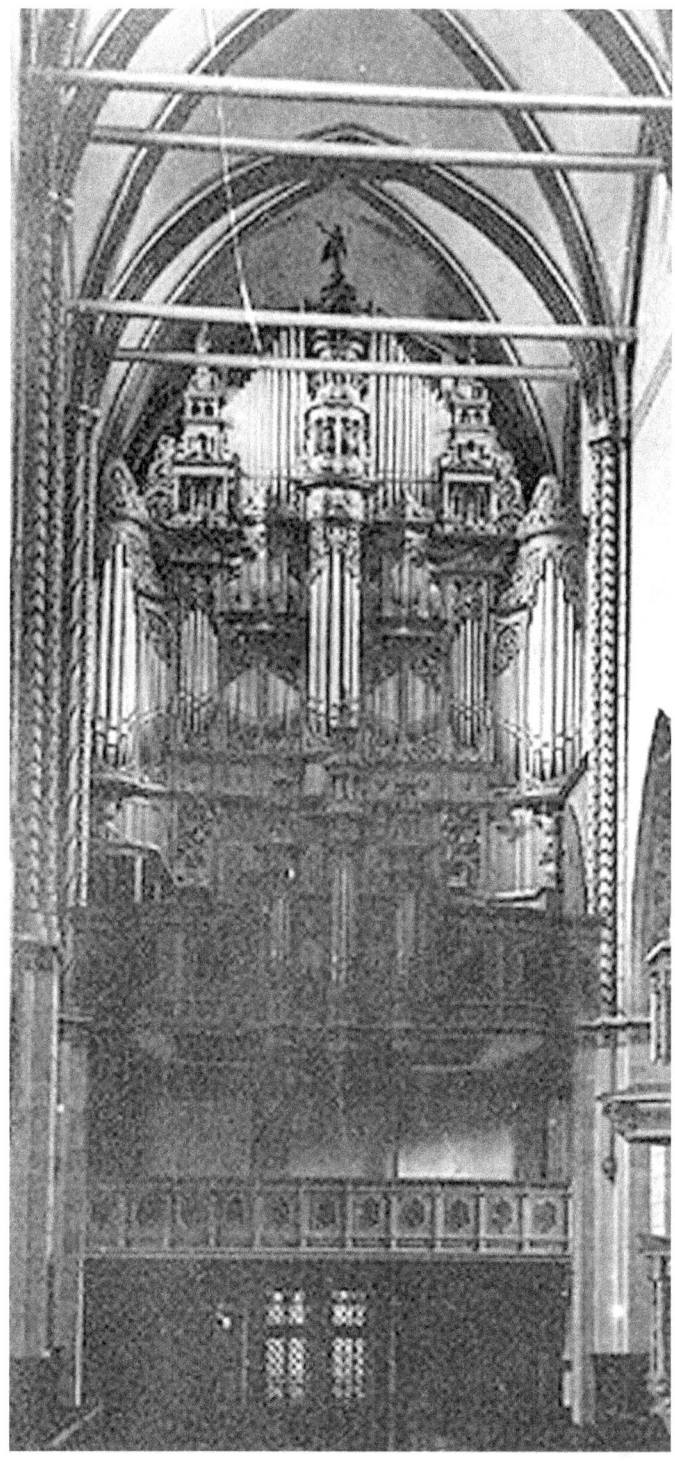

She signed her diary as *Maude,* her middle name, after that.

While in Germany, Magda Maude had been taught music on an older organ, manufactured before electricity, when bellows were used to pump air into the reservoir.

> *My fingers are simply itching to play the organ again. Oh! I attended Mass at St. Patrick's Cathedral today — such a magnificent Gothic Revival Style structure. I vow to never walk through the doors of any church other than a Catholic one from now on, forever and ever!*

At the age of twelve, she was one of the first students admitted into the school adjacent to St. Patrick's.

> *1885 — The Statue of Liberty arrived today, in 350 pieces, on the French Ship* Isere. *I will watch them reconstruct it, and someday climb to the top!*

Dainie took a break and sat down with me. Her mother had shared as much as she could remember with her about Magda. She had gone to court to retrieve her German family surname after the death of her husband in 1933. I thought of her as one of the original Women's Libbers and had no doubt that she had, in fact, reached the top of the Statue of Liberty, probably more than once in her life. She was one determined lady, especially if she could make music come from an organ that was no longer assembled!

"She played the great organ at St. Patrick's in recital concerts many times, according to my mother," Dainie said, "and occasionally filled in for the regular organist during church services."

"Good! Her itchy fingers finally got their wish," I said.

"Yep, big time, I'd say. Magda's husband died somewhere around 1933, and their daughter insisted she move to Tennessee to live with her. She met my mother then, because we lived just a couple houses down the street. Magda told my mother she really missed what she called the Big Apple energy. She searched through Nashville for a Catholic church with a pipe organ, but couldn't find one."

"Is that when she started attending the Baptist church?"

"Well, yes. Mother made arrangements for Magda to play in a recital at our First Baptist Church near White House. After that, they invited her to fill in for our organist ever so often, and then she got the permanent position a couple years after that. Mother said even though Magda preferred the Catholic way of worship, by that time she believed it's not your religion, but the music in your heart that matters to God.

"Mother and Magda had quickly become close, and Magda made lots of other friends there at First Baptist. Oh, and attendance on Sundays picked up right away. That Magda, she had a distinctive style. Like a snake charmer, just lured that religion right out of your heart, sent it straight up to the Lord. When she pulled out all the stops, those old pipes *moved*, and you just had to sing!"

"Why are the old organ parts in storage?"

"Magda died in 1950, right at the console. We tried to find somebody to replace her, but that old gal was one-of-a-kind. No one ever played it like she did, but the congregation went on just the same. Then, in 1955, the church was struck by lightning and burned — ruined. But the organ wasn't damaged, not so much as a warped pipe! The minister said it was a miracle, so they dismantled and stored it in an old barn. I guess they'd planned to put it in the new church when it got built, but that never happened. A few years later, the barn got torn down because of the new Interstate, so the organ pieces were stuck into the storage shed back there in that field. It was a shame, really, to let it sit like that."

"I guess Magda thought so too, huh?"

Dainie smiled. "Yeah. Ya know what's funny . . . there was like a visible straight line where the fire stopped, just inches from the organ. Mother told me she knew Magda's ghost was there, even then, protecting it. I guess that's why, when I heard the music here, I figured right away it had to be her a playin' it."

Mamoo's Haunted Dollhouse

As told by Greta S. Cooper-Coe

My grandmother lives in a dollhouse. I inherited it when she died, and that's when the *real* fun began, because she moved right in.

When I was a child, MaMoo took me on a weekend trip to a charming tourist area in Brown County, Indiana. The quaint city of Nashville was full of gift shops, specialty restaurants and homemade-candy stores. It was the most magical town I had ever seen in my nine years of life.

When we stepped through the entrance of a place on Jefferson Street called Jeepers Dollhouse Miniatures, the enchantment intensified. Shelves were laden with meticulously finished dollhouses of all shapes, sizes and colors: a pink Victorian with white gingerbread trim; a yellow French Chalet with blue, old-world window boxes; a sand-beige Contemporary with skylights; and a delightful maple tree-house growing right in the middle of the shop.

Display cabinets bulged with miniatures: kitchen tables and chairs; sofas and loveseats, toilets and vanities; tiny plates of watermelon, lobster, bagels and smoked salmon. Little seasonal items such as greeting cards, Christmas trees, birthday cakes and Halloween skeletons. Scale building supplies like roofing shingles, paint, wood floors and lighting kits. You name it — Jeepers had it in stock.

We both fell in love with the Contemporary. It consisted of four large rooms and a loft, a spiral staircase, vaulted ceilings with four huge skylights and angle-shaped windows. On the portico was parked a small-scale, baby-blue, 1958 Chevy. I seriously wanted that house.

After much thought, I finally decided on the light blue Vermont Farmhouse because it had seven rooms, and I had five of them decorated in my mind already. MaMoo, fixated on the Contemporary, bought it for herself, although it had been her intention to buy only one dollhouse — for me. She purchased the kits and we built the houses ourselves. So, there we were, right in the thick of a new hobby — doll-housing.

I watched with delight as she created a vacation beach home out of hers. It was so authentic — anyone would have loved to live in it. She put red tile flooring in the living room with mission-style furniture, and lots of tropical plants, but she didn't dare add a television because she didn't want to watch TV while on vacation. When we played with her beach house, it really was like being on holiday.

My grandfather put the house on a large craft board, and he fashioned the Gulf Coast out of spackling, sculpting

lifelike waves just outside the front door of their beach house. He used several shades of blue paint, the realism of which was fully convincing. MaMoo glued sand we'd brought home from the Bahamas up to the ocean's edge.

She helped me furnish my two-story and offered me some decorating tips, too, such as the tropical forest theme for my upstairs attic-recreation room: black textured carpet with a leopard-design area rug, a futon covered with silk zebra-printed fabric (hand-sewn by MaMoo) and jungle wallpaper. The room eventually housed a wide-screen television because my dolls just had to have it, don't you know. MaMoo added a mini bowl of popcorn, two bottles of soda pop, a remote-control device and a set of stacking tables to satisfy my miniature television-watchers.

Every Christmas I found dollhouse goodies in my stocking — not from Santa — but from MaMoo, and I did the same for her. We continued this tradition well into my adult life, even after I was married with children of my own.

MaMoo lived to be a very old woman, and, when she passed away, she left me a personal letter full of advice for daily living. *Just in case you need it,* she'd instructed. I refer to it quite often, even now after all these years.

She also left me something else — her Contemporary Beach House! Right away, I placed it on a table next to my Vermont Farmhouse. The day after her funeral, I unpacked her miniatures and put them in carefully, just the way she had always done.

We lived close to the U.S. Space and Rocket Center in Huntsville, Alabama. While she was raising my dad and his brothers, she worked as a civil servant for the Rocket Center as a typist. She was obsessed with rocket figurines and had a collection of them on display in her real-life house.

She managed to locate a few miniature spaceships, as well, and had set them on the fireplace mantel of her dollhouse, tallest on the right — shortest on the left.

In her imagination, the house was on a Pensacola beach, and she said the winters could get pretty nippy in the Florida Panhandle. She always said that's why she had a fireplace in her dollhouse. But I believe she secretly wanted to hang Christmas stockings there.

It seemed to me, the rockets looked better with the tallest one in the middle, and the shorter ones on either side, so that's the way I set them up. After all, it *was* my dollhouse now, so I thought I could do what I wanted.

A few days later, I noticed that the rockets had been moved into MaMoo's preferred style. Naturally, I blamed Ella, my three-year old, although I had instructed her not to touch anything. She insisted she hadn't. I wanted to believe her, so…perhaps my husband was the culprit?

He blinked a few times at the suggestion. "Maybe it's haunted," he said with a laugh. "I do believe I saw the lights flicker on and off last night."

"Yeah, right," I said.

The next morning, I noticed my petite, red coffeemaker on the stove of her beach house, with a mug that read *GRANDMA* sitting on the kitchen table. A plate of cookies sat alongside the cup.

Those items were *mine,* and I had not displayed them like that, so I figured, once again, that either Ella or my husband had played with the houses. I couldn't blame them, really, because the beach house was just too inviting.

Still, I considered my husband's ghost theory. I rearranged the accessories and peered into the beach house. I whispered, "MaMoo . . . are you in there?" Nothing happened. I don't know what I expected.

Each morning after that, for two weeks, I checked out the beach house kitchen, and I found the coffeemaker and the *GRANDMA* mug on the table. Sometimes there would be a quart of milk and a bowl of cereal, or bacon and eggs, and oftentimes lox and bagels, which had been one of her favorites. By that time, I took it for granted that my husband was playing a joke on me.

Then he took a two-day business trip.

I brought Ella into bed with me the first night to keep me company, and Eric, the baby, slept in his crib, as usual.

Come morning, I found the coffeepot situation to be the same, and that was probably my first inkling that, indeed, MaMoo's ghost was *living* in her beach house! There could have been no other logical explanation.

Then I did some serious thinking. I recalled our many trips to the beach together. MaMoo loved the feel of sand between her toes, and the warmth of the sun beating down on her skin. Two or three times each year, we drove 5-1/2 hours to Pensacola, rented a beach cabana and had some of the best times of our lives.

She used to say she wished she could live forever at the beach. I told her I wished I could, too. When she built her beach house in miniature, she said she dreamed of living in it. I felt the same way. But this . . . this was too weird for words.

When my husband got back in town, I told him my suspicion. He blinked a few times, because that's what he always did when he was trying to think. He smiled, and said, "How cool that you still have MaMoo; you haven't lost her at all, Sweetheart, now have you?"

I agreed — it was pretty amazing.

~*~

My birthday was coming, and I was dreading it. I awakened early that morning and glanced at the clock; I would be forty in just under two hours. Gloomy, I fixed myself a cup of hot tea and sat down in the family room. I heard a scratching noise and glanced over at the dollhouses.

I could hardly believe my eyes! My Vermont Farmhouse's tiny mailbox was stuffed full of presents! I placed the packages on my little dining room table. MaMoo had given me a miniature birthday cake, red balloons, and a glitter card on my tenth birthday, so I removed them from the kitchen cabinet and put them with the presents. I couldn't wait for MaMoo's birthday the following month, so I could give *her* a surprise party!

Sometimes I wonder if she hangs around Earth so she can observe our holidays. She was always celebrating something or other when she was in her body. She has a ceramic jack-o-lantern with a miniscule light bulb inside, and when Halloween rolls around, that cute little guy still lights up at night. Of course, I find her fragile, plastic spider web in one corner of the kitchen doorway, and the Trick or Treat bag she was always fond of, usually on the coffee table. Christmas used to be her favorite time of year, but now I think it's Halloween. After all, she is officially a ghost.

Fourth of July is always interesting at MaMoo's beach house. She hangs a wind sock, designed to look like the American Flag, from the porch overhang, and she's accumulated a nice assortment of fireworks. I just hope she doesn't accidently burn down the house with those sparklers. She did that once, many years ago, to a real-life house she had. What a mess! My dad always said she did it on purpose so she could redecorate, but she insisted it was an accident.

I bought her a miniature fire extinguisher, just in case.

MaMoo put the Contemporary's loft to work as an attic, where she stored all of her seasonal items and a wooden trunk with old quilts and toys.

On Thanksgiving Day, like clockwork, she takes her Christmas tree out of the attic and sets it up in her living room. She rearranges her furniture, hangs hand-knitted stockings on the mantle and puts a variety of wrapped packages under the tree. Her poinsettia plant appears on the bedroom nightstand, and a wreath shows up on the front door.

We exchange presents at Christmas, tiny boxes hand-wrapped, empty of course, but, like my grandmother always said, it's the thought that counts.

I was so excited at first about my grandmother's ghost that I told everyone about her, but they usually looked at me like I was crazy.

My friends still insist I imagine these occurrances. My dad makes fun of me when I tell him his mother's ghost lives with me, but he's a stand-up comic, so he makes fun of pretty much everybody and gets paid for it. The only one who's really onboard is Ella. She gets it.

So, now I rarely say anything about MaMoo to outsiders. But it's nice to know she's there.

She has a little clothesline strung out along the back yard. I never know what I'll find hanging on it. More often than not, it's her aqua, polka-dot bathing suit. Sometimes I notice a pair of men's Birkenstock sandals in the sand, next to the chaise lounge, so I suppose she has a visitor now and again. I assume it's Grandpa, but I'm not one to judge.

The game of croquet seems to be one of her specialties.

Every once in a while I have to retrieve the balls when they fall to the floor. Go figure. I'm just glad she's living the good life.

Sometimes I'll find a little letter in my dollhouse mailbox, a list of things she wants. She asks for expensive stuff, too, like Godiva Chocolates, beef tenderloin, and avacados. All that rich food can kill a person, but I guess MaMoo doesn't have to worry about that. One year she requested Christmas tree ornaments. I guess she'd dropped and broken some of her vintage glass ones. I call Jeepers Miniatures and order whatever she needs.

I've even bought some things that I, myself, like, such as a surfboard, snorkle equipment, and a hammock for in-between the palm trees right outside her kitchen window, just in case I am lucky enough to move in with her someday in that wonderful beach house.